Published in 2023 by FeedARead.com Publishing
Copyright © Judith Arnopp2023

First edition

A CIP catalogue record for this title is available from the
British Library.

Edited by Cas Peace
Cover by @CoverGirl: AdobeStock,knight with scars
By Andrey Kiselev
Marcus Stone, The Royal Nursery 1548 via WikimediaCommons

A MATTER
OF
FAITH:
The Days of the Phoenix

JUDITH ARNOPP

For Ben,
my noble prince

Acknowledgements

I am always at a loss when it comes to thanking those who have assisted me in producing a readable book. To name everyone will take up pages so please forgive me if I miss anyone. There are my parents, who instilled in me a love of books and history. There are my teachers who encouraged my love of learning, particularly my university professors who took the time to convince a painfully shy student that she was good enough to pursue a career in writing. Then, there is my team of beta readers, and my guinea pig/husband John, who does the initial read throughs, spotting typos, inconsistencies, and sometimes even praises the good bits.

Writing is a lonely job; I am always beset by insecurity, fraud syndrome, inferiority. My fellow writers on social media help me overcome this: in particular, The Coffee Pot gang, who support, encourage, share, read and review and prop up my flagging ego. I couldn't do any of this without my editor, Cas Peace, who refines and tames my work into a readable state. But most of all, I appreciate my readers, especially those who are so patient when I overshoot deadlines, constantly sing my praises on social media, and leave me such astonishingly lovely reviews. I shall endeavour to pen the next volume in this trilogy in record time.

Please note: The thoughts and opinions expressed in this historical fiction novel are not the author's own.

January 1533 – Whitehall Palace

"Anne!" I jump awake, stare blindly into the darkness, battling with the vivid dream. I long for the onset of dawn. I've had little rest; all night I've twitched and fidgeted, thrown off the covers and dragged them back again, turned my pillow, drained my water jug. I have lost count of the times my attendant, who this night is Henry Norris, has raised his head from his own pillow to enquire after my health, and each time I snarled at him to leave me in peace.

The cold, dark, damp January night drips slowly into morning. January is a month I always abhor; the short dreary days and long dreary nights are devoid of cheer, and sometimes it seems, even devoid of hope. Every January is the same; the courtiers grow restless, petty squabbles mushroom into feuds, and light attraction inflates into heated passion. The poets mark May as the month of love but if you tally the number of bastards born in October, I'll lay good coin on January being the month of lust.

This year it will certainly be my month of love for, in a short time, with just a few gentlemen for company, I will quietly leave my chamber to meet Anne in the chapel. And there, I will make her my wife.

I have waited so long to have her and, although I now have full knowledge of her and she carries my son in her womb, in the eyes of God she does not yet belong to me. But this is about to change.

I roll onto my side, punch the pillow, and imagine the unmitigated joy of having her in my bed, legitimately, every night for the rest of my life. Beneath the covers, I move my fingers, counting forward the months until the time our prince is estimated to be born. September, Anne thinks.

It seems such a long way away.

1

My groom of the chamber, Norris, snorts and mutters in his sleep and I curl my lip, silently begrudging his peaceful slumber when I have had little. If only I could let go of tomorrow and sleep, sleep until my wedding day.

With a loud huff, I thump the pillow again before giving up and throwing back the covers. Careful not to wake Norris, I cross the shadowy chamber to the window. The glass is misted with condensation, obscuring my view, and rubbing it with my sleeve affords little improvement. The catch is stiff, necessitating force, and I pull so hard my elbow strikes the shutter and sends it crashing against the wall. Norris leaps from slumber and stands befuddled before me.

"Is all well, Your Majesty?"

He scratches his head, dislodging his cap and leaving his hair spiked.

"It is almost time, Norris. I can sleep no more. Fetch me water that I may wash."

Dispensing with the usual ceremony, he helps me clean my face and hands, and assists me into the warm thick velvet clothes selected for my wedding. I reposition the collar – a collar of blackwork sewn by the hand of Kate. I push her begrudging image away and allow him to fasten my doublet. When my sword is swinging comfortably at my hip, Norris himself dresses hastily, pulling on his hose and shrugging into the doublet he wore yesterday. A bell rings, marking dawn. It is time to go. I shiver as a ripple of trepidation creeps over me, but I refuse to pay it attention. It is natural to be nervous when all one's worldly dreams are about to come true.

"So," I say. "We are ready."

He smiles, nods encouragingly as he ensures all my laces are tied and my linen tucked in.

"Your Majesty, may I wish you every happiness?"

"You may, Norris. And you may also wish me a son … in due course."

"Of course, Sire. That wish is in my every prayer, as it is in everybody's."

We tread quietly along the corridor where the guards are leaning half asleep against the wall. They rouse sluggishly and straighten at our approach, no doubt surprised at my early rising.

Anne! She will be waiting for me. I quicken my pace, turn a corner, and spy a light shining from beyond the chapel door, a murmur of voices from within. Has she arrived before me?

We have told only a few friends of our plan to wed this morn. There are many who believe I am not yet free to marry but they must be made to understand that my marriage to Kate was never a true marriage – it was a mistake, invalid and unbinding in God's eyes. For more than twenty years, I have lived a lie.

In my heart, I know I was meant to wait for Anne. I know she was sent to me by God to be the vessel for my heart's one desire ... a son to follow after. A son for England.

A shadow crosses the threshold and Brereton puts his head around the door, his face stretching into smiles when he notes my approach.

"There you are, Your Majesty. We feared you'd changed your mind."

We keep our laughter low as I duck beneath the lintel and make the *signum crucis* before the altar. There is an air of expectation, suppressed excitement infusing the usual calm of the chapel. I take a deep breath, exhale slowly, and close my eyes as I attempt to master my nerves. My habitual confidence is melting away; inwardly I writhe with fear that she will not come. But she would never flee, she loves me ... unless ... ? Only Anne could make me this unsure.

Suppose she has taken flight; suppose it has all been a game? She could have changed her mind, left court during the night, galloped away, taken ship and crossed the sea! She could disappear into the wildness of the world, never to be found. Panic squirms in my belly. I bite my lip, shuffle my feet, my tremulous breath audible to everyone.

"She will be here anon, Sire. Do not worry." Thomas Henage nods encouragement. I straighten my shoulders, grasp the furred collar of my coat.

"Oh, I am not worried, gentlemen, not worried in the least."

But I am.

The lightening dawn filters through the slit window, a draught blows in from the passage, the torches flicker, the altar candles dance. Still, she does not come.

I wait.

Why does she tarry so? I'd have thought she'd come early, impatient for our union. Is she doing this on purpose? Does she take pleasure in making me sweat?

My fear is just dissolving into annoyance when I hear the sound of a footstep. A light step, the swish of a petticoat. I stand up straight, arrange my face into a welcome, but my hopes are dashed again when the doorway reveals Dr Lee, come to perform the ceremony. He is followed by a blurry-eyed choirboy, his silk robes a little long and trailing across the floor.

"Your Majesty. Good morrow. I think I heard the ladies approaching as I turned the corner."

Relief floods through me. I nod to the priest to take his position. The boy begins to sing, his initial sleepy croakiness clearing to sweetness. I turn toward a sound at the door and there she is, as radiant as a new day in spring. She has evidently passed a restful night for she glows like an angel of heaven. She bows her head, genuflects hastily in front of the rood before approaching the altar where I wait.

"Anne!"

Her smile is warm as she glides toward me, her fingers slide into my palm as I lean forward to kiss her cheek. She is real, not an angel; she is solid and earthy and mine. I wish I could stay here, her scent in my nose, the taste of her skin on my tongue, but Norris clears his throat.

"Time is passing, Sire."

We pull our faces apart and stand together, hand in hand at the altar where Dr Rowlands Lee awaits us. His upper lip is beaded with sweat, and his hands tremble as he opens his book and calls down a blessing on those gathered.

He opens his mouth to speak.

4

"Y-Your Majesty, before we begin … you are required to produce the papal licence allowing this marriage."

I stiffen, blood rushing to my head.

"I do not have it to hand; I left it in Cromwell's keeping. I will show it to you later. Get on with it, man; day is fast approaching."

Dr Lee's face blanches.

"It really is a requirement, Your Majesty …"

"Damn you! Get on with it."

He quails beneath my outrage, fumbles with the pages of his book and makes the sign of the cross over those gathered.

I am lying. I have no such papal licence. I am the king. I do not need one; a monkey would recognise the illegality of my union with Kate. Thankfully, he dare not argue with his king but takes a deep breath and speaks the words that will bind Anne to me before God and before the church.

"*In nòmine Patris, et Fìlii, et Spìritus Sancti.*"

I clutch Anne's hand, willing the fellow to hurry, willing the time to pass until he says the words that confirm us man and wife.

I close my eyes, the scent of incense fills my head, the song of the choirboy is high and pure, and Anne's fingers are tight in my palm. It is finally happening, yet even now I do not believe it. This day has been so long in coming, we have wasted so many years: years spent wooing, persuading, fighting the Pope, fighting Kate, fighting my own friends.

Just a few moments more, I tell myself, just a few moments more and she will be mine. She will be my wife, and queen in all but name.

As Dr Lee's words unite us in marriage, the sun rises in glory. It breaks from the clouds as if in evidence of heavenly approval; an ethereal light streams into the chapel and falls upon us.

When I turn to kiss her, my head swims, my heart pounds as if it will burst from my chest. She is my wife. Our lips part and I pull away, but I do not let go but keep a firm hold on her hand.

5

"Behold, gentlemen," I say, feeling as if my heart will burst. "I give you your Queen."

Our friends cluster around us, expressing joy, good wishes. I beam upon the company, high and low, and notice Anne's servant rubbing her arms and stamping her feet, and for the first time I notice the frigid temperature of the chapel. I hold up a hand, severing their chatter and dampening the mood of celebration.

"Remember, you must speak of this to no one, not even your wives and sweethearts, or any other members of the queen's household. We all know how keen this court is for gossip, but I must first break news of this to my council ..."

When I wake at first light, Anne's hair is tangled in my beard, the warm globe of her belly cradled in my palms. I do not move, even when my legs become cramped, and the tickling of her hair becomes unbearable. I am happy, I think, happy for the first time in almost twenty years. I never want this feeling to end. I want this moment to go on and on forever. My wife in my arms and my son alive beneath my palms but, even as I wish it, I know that perfect moments cannot last. All I can do is cling to the memory of this first morning, the first morning of an eternity of joy.

My mind drifts to all the changes I will make now Anne is my queen. I must punish those who stood against us, reward those who gave their support. I will make Cranmer Archbishop of Canterbury, and that fellow Cromwell, I will raise him up too, even higher than I have already. He is clever, he is cunning, and he is determined; a loyal servant despite his lowly beginnings.

It is the lordly ones I must be wary of; those of the blood who lust after power, one eye on the crown, the other on their own deficiencies. Anne's coronation must be organised too; I plan a grand affair so the world may look upon her beauty, her fertility, and finally understand why I was constrained to set Kate aside.

Anne shifts and mutters in her sleep and I hold my breath for fear of waking her. She exhales, and when she begins to breathe deeply again, I relax, relishing the solidity of her body in my arms, the silkiness of a strand of her dark hair that is tickling my nose. But I will have to rouse her soon, the close stool is calling me, and later on this morning I have a meeting with the Privy Council, where I will set all these plans in motion. My Anne, my glorious Anne.

I kiss her hair, close my eyes and send up yet another silent prayer of thanks that she is mine at last. Marriage to Anne has made me anew. I can forget the worries and uncertainties of my time with Kate; the future now holds only good things, only love and success and sons, so many sons. The child that is thriving in Anne's belly now is merely the first.

The chamber door opens and Cut and Ball come tumbling into the room, with Anne's pug, Purkoy, yapping at their heels. The chamber erupts into a cacophony of barking. Anne groans, rolls away from me and buries her head beneath her pillow.

"Shut them up, Henry, my head!"

"The dogs are as eager to be up and out as I am for the chamber pot." Playfully, I slap Anne's bottom and she squeals, her dishevelled head appearing from the depths of the bed.

"How dare you, Sir!" she cries with pretended outrage. She rolls over and sits up, dragging the covers to her chin, and pats the counterpane, encouraging Purkoy to jump onto the bed. He leaps and hops in vain attempt but is far too small, so I scoop him up and drop him into her lap where the beast licks her face in a paroxysm of ecstasy.

If my need for the pot wasn't so pressing, I'd be jealous.

Behind the screen, I sigh with pleasure as I let go an arc of golden piss.

"Shall we hunt today, husband?" Anne calls from the bed.

"Later, by all means, but I have a council meeting this morning. We need to set the arrangements for your coronation in motion."

7

"We do indeed. I've a royal wardrobe to arrange."

Purkoy has taken up residence on my pillow and has one leg behind his ear while he nibbles at a flea. Anne is sitting up, both hands on her belly which will soon be as round as a globe.

"Will you still love me if I grow as fat as a cardinal?"

Something stabs beneath my ribs, but I refuse to be downhearted by reminders of Wolsey. Signalling for the page to summon my gentlemen, I turn to face her.

"I'll still love you, my sweet, if you grow as fat as the fattest swine in our kingdom."

"I am tiny as yet; I hope by the time of my coronation I will not be too large to lie on my face before the altar."

"If you are, I will have them dig a hole in the nave floor to accommodate your belly. Ah, Norris, there you are. Are you ready with my toilette? I will come with you now. Make haste, sweetheart, or you will miss the best part of the day."

As I quit the chamber, I turn for one last look, in time to see Anne take hold of her dog and slide back beneath the covers.

*

"You should insist she comes; it is impudent of her to refuse!"

"Brandon says Mary is sick." I turn away and continue to feed crumbs to my songbirds. Anne's disgruntlement at my sister's decline of the invitation to the coronation is boring me. She plumps onto the window seat, folds her arms and frowns into the distance.

"I don't believe she is sick at all. I've not forgotten how she was also conveniently too ill to attend our wedding. This is just another snub. She hates me."

"Mary would never lie. Her love for me would bring her even against her will. Kate is her friend …"

"And that friendship is the very thing that makes her hate me."

8

I sigh and turn back to her, misliking what I see. Anger makes her ugly. Her whole countenance darkens, her eyes narrow, and the parallel lines between her brows deepen. I want her to smile again.

"There is no need to be so upset. You should think of the child."

Her hands move to her belly. Her body deflates but discontent continues to mar her face.

"If you loved me, you'd force her to come; you'd force her to honour me."

"Anne." I sit beside her and take her hands. "I know Mary better than anyone. The more I insist she does something, the stronger she will resist. In time, your sweet nature will win her friendship. If you are kind to her, make yourself agreeable, all will be …"

"How can I possibly make myself agreeable if she continues to refuse to accept me? If she were anybody else, you'd throw her in the Tower!"

"It won't be forever. She will recover with the spring weather and return to court. Why don't you write her a letter, tell her of your disappointment that she cannot attend? If it doesn't change her mind, at least it will be proof of your love for her."

Anne huffs and scowls, only cheering a little when Purkoy is brought back from his walk. He immediately leaps onto her lap and while Anne lavishes kisses on him, I continue to feed my birds.

As I feed them titbits through the bars of the cages that line the chamber window, my mind drifts to other matters. The arrangements for the coronation are underway and it is costing me a goodly amount, but Anne is worth it. Cost what it will, I am determined to show the world that she is not only my lawful wife but also my queen.

Anne has been feverish with excitement for weeks, determined that each detail of her coronation will be perfect. The route she will take to the abbey has been carefully planned, as have the clothes she will wear, the women who will attend her. If she has anything to do with it, everything is going to be flawless.

Before her big day, we spend a night together in the Tower where the royal apartments have been newly refurbished in her honour. It has been hard for me for we have not lain together as man and wife for months for fear of harming the child, but I try to calm her ragged nerves.

She nestles into my shoulder while I stroke her hair and it seems as if my fingers absorb her agitation. I should have remembered that all this is new to her; she has never been the object of ceremony before. Not just the eyes of England will be upon her but those of Europe too. The court is filled with foreign diplomats and ambassadors, all come here to see for themselves the beauty of the new queen and take the news back to their masters. Anne is aware of this and deeply worried about taking a wrong step, making herself look foolish in the eyes of the world. Witnessing momentous events is vastly different to being the centre of them.

I whisper to her of other coronations, that of my mother and father, my grandfather Edward IV, but I do not speak of my own for Kate was there with me, and I am learning it is best not to mention her name.

"Of course, the crown of Richard III was snatched from his head and placed on my father's while he was still on the battlefield, but his official coronation was, by all accounts, a vast affair. My mother's – somewhat delayed – ceremony was not quite as splendid but I remember her telling me that when she entered the abbey it felt as though all her ancestors had crowded into the nave to watch. Funnily enough, I felt that too … when it was my turn. It was not just the eyes of the world but … you will think me foolish."

When Anne makes no reply, I glance down and discover she has drifted off to sleep. I suppress a chuckle and wonder how long I have been talking to myself. The weight of her head leaves me cramped and uncomfortable, but I do not disturb her. She needs her rest, if only for the sake of the child. While she sleeps, her gentle snores are like those of a puppy. I play with her hair, whisper secrets to my unborn son and dream happily of his first tooth, his first step, his first pony.

The night is long and I rouse often, my dreams wild and discomforting, but when we are woken early by the chamberers, I wish there was no need to rise. My head is as thick and heavy as if I'd spent the night in the stews. Another hour or two of sleep would seem a luxury.

As soon as she opens her eyes, Anne begins to fret about tiny details.

"How heavy is St Edward's crown? Suppose I drop the orb or mishandle the sceptre? Suppose I say the wrong thing …"

I close my ears.

"I will leave you to prepare," I say, taking her hand and kissing it. "Just focus. All is in hand, the plans are set, and everyone knows what they are doing. Just relax and let it happen. Just think: the next time I see you will be at the abbey; the deed will have been done and you will be Queen of England."

"Oh Henry, I do hope I do not disappoint you."

"As if you ever could. You were born for this day."

Passionately, I kiss her cold fingers again and run a hand across her belly in farewell to my son.

After my fast is broken and my toilette is complete, I travel by barge to Westminster Abbey and take my place behind a screen, high up in the nave where I will not be seen but will enjoy a bird's eye view of the proceedings. While I wait, the congregation slowly grows and I scrutinise each new arrival, taking note of who is present and, more importantly, who is not.

Mary, to my sorrow, has not relented, but I spy Brandon seated with the other nobles to honour me and no doubt hoping to curry favour with Anne. I scan the crowd for Thomas More and frown when I realise he is missing, but I am not surprised. He has never sought to conceal his love for Kate, which clearly exceeds any affection he ever held for me. My heart fills with sorrow at his absence.

I've valued his friendship since I was a boy. Although he has often frustrated me with his intractability, I had hoped that in this matter, which is so close to my heart, he would at least make an outward show of support. Anne's parents are there and … her sister, Mary, but her brother, George, of course is on a mission overseas, doing my bidding, serving his king. Anne begged me to summon him home so he might share in her triumph but … sometimes even I lack the power to grant her every wish.

A blast of trumpets signals Anne's imminent arrival and the congregation stands with a clatter of feet and a wave of conversation. I also rise, cling to the latticed screen and peer through a gap in the design, craning my neck for a better view.

I've not seen her in full regalia before. When my eyes light upon her, I catch my breath, surprised at her regal bearing as she processes toward the dais, her purple ermined robe trailing softly over the carpet. She keeps her head straight, her eye on the throne and, to all intent and purpose, she is perfectly composed. Only I note her clenched fists, the tightness of her jaw, and understand the fear that leaps and twists in her heart.

While Kate took the ceremony in her stride, as comfortable with royal ritual as only one born to it can be, Anne is fearful. For all her new title of Marchioness of Pembroke, in her heart and mind she still thinks herself a private gentlewoman of middling status, but no one would know. She is tall and gracious, obediently following Cranmer's all but invisible instructions as to what to do next.

She moves slowly toward the altar, and with the aid of the Duchess of Norfolk, prostrates herself before the cross. The nave falls silent, only the odd cough or shuffle of feet disturbing the solemnity of the moment. This is the part of the ceremony that Anne has worried about the most, fearful that the child will be crushed or the pressure on her bladder will make her wet the holy tiles.

Cranmer begins to intone a prayer, his voice rising and falling, drawing the rapt attention of those gathered. He holds us all captive. He is a good man who does my bidding. A few days ago, he made a declaration that my marriage to Kate was no marriage and thus my union with Anne was legal in the eyes of God and his church. And this day, he raises her even higher – she is no longer my concubine, no longer merely my wife, but is my queen - the Queen of England.

At last, the prayer ends, and I realise I have been holding my breath. I watch as Anne is assisted to her feet. She looks relieved to be upright again. She flashes a smile at her step-grandmother as the duchess rearranges her skirts. Then she stands tall as the soaring voices of the choir wash over her in a *te deum*, so high and pure that the hairs on my arms and the back of my neck rise, and a tear moistens my eye.

I wish I were there with her, at her side, that I might share the moment of her glory. I feel like a spy, a fly on the wall, a sparrow on the rafters. I am unaccustomed to being closeted away, out of sight. It is strange that all eyes are on Anne while I am invisible. I cough loudly, to see who harkens to it, but only Brandon raises his eyes and smiles. He knows I am there, but he cannot see me, but I am gratified that he noticed me, just the same.

I turn my attention back to Anne, just in time to see Cranmer raise St Edward's crown high. Everyone looks upon it, acknowledges the power contained within. He then slowly lowers the coronet, and when he rests it on her brow, a murmur runs across the nave, a relaxing of tension.

Keeping her head still for fear of dislodging it, Anne looks about the congregation, her eyes creeping to where she knows I will be watching. Although she cannot see me, she smiles, a queen triumphant, and her smile is for me alone. We have done it!

"Anne!"

My attendant jumps when I speak her name aloud. I cling to the screen, my heart racing at the power of the moment. I have done it. I have beaten all opposition. Anne is my wife. She is Queen of England and there is nothing the

Pope, nor Kate, nor Spain, nor Fisher nor Thomas More can do about it.

<u>25th June 1533</u>

I remain in high spirits long after the celebrations have ended, and so does my queen. Anne immediately sets about making changes to the décor in her chambers, ordering new hangings, lavish cushions and seat covers. Her attentions make the chambers gay, such as they never were during Kate's pious days. I push the thought away. Not only is it disrespectful to my new queen but it always spoils my day if I dwell on Kate in her remote palace or think of Mary alone and probably grieving for both of us.

I focus my thoughts on happier things: turn to the boy that will soon be born, to the summer that is just beginning, to the future with Anne where one son will quickly follow another. A royal nursery full to overflowing with princes, princesses – the future of my dynasty bolstered by royal marriages, foreign alliances. With such certainties in my head, I stride along the corridors of Westminster with a smile as wide as the Thames.

"It is a fine day. The women are happy with their cushions and coverlets, we should leave them to it and spend the afternoon it in the tiltyard!" I cry. "Where is Brandon? Have you seen him today?"

Brereton looks up from the chess game he and Norris are engaged in.

"He is at his estates, Your Majesty, don't you remember?"

"Oh yes, of course."

I had forgotten. I bite my lip. Since Anne's coronation, Brandon slips away from court at every opportunity. I fear he will never accept her as queen, and never even try to like her. Well, I don't need him. I never have done. Not really.

"No matter," I say. "I will beat you instead, Norris, what say you to that?"

"I say you are probably right, Your Majesty!"

Abandoning his game of chess, he stands up and we laugh before taking leave of the women and making our way to the tiltyard. As we are crossing the gardens, a footstep sounds on the gravel behind us. We pause and turn to find a boy who is sheepishly holding out a letter. He bows as I take it from him and stare at the seal.

It is from Suffolk.

As I make to break the wax I hear another footstep, more urgent this time. I look up to find Thomas Cromwell, hat in hand, looking uncomfortable and rather pale.

"Cromwell? What can I do for you?"

A ridiculous question since he is clearly here to do my bidding.

"Your Majesty …"

His eyes are on the letter in my hand. "I - I suspect you might wish to … open that in private."

I scowl, fear stabbing in my gut. Briskly, I turn from my companions, walk a few paces away and break the seal. Cromwell is at my elbow, but he gives me space, looking away from me while I read and, when I have done, speaks to the flowering shrub at the side of the path.

"I am so sorry, Your Majesty, you have my … condolence."

My hand trembles as I reread the letter and force the dancing sentences to make sense. I cannot seem to catch my breath; it leaves my body, my legs turn to string, and I utter a sound unlike any I've uttered before.

"No."

Pain is like a lance in my chest, and I am staggered by it. With a grunt of concern, Cromwell takes my arm and assists me to an arboured seat where, among the roses and honeysuckle, I read the note again. I read it several times before my shock at the contents abates enough for me to speak.

"My sister is dead."

Is it me who utters those words?

"Yes, Your Majesty. I … You have my sincere condolences."

He said that before. Can he not think of anything better? Such a trite sentence for so immense a feeling. It is no help to anyone, let alone the king of England who has lost his favourite sister.

I look down at my hand, which still clutches the message, and clench my fist to make the trembling stop. It cannot be true. Mary cannot be *dead*. Not my brave, vital, rude, obstinate little sister. She is the only person who … the only person who *knows* me. She never stopped knowing me or treating me as the scared little boy who shared her nursery. What am I supposed to do without her? How can I go on?

A sob escapes me. I fumble for a kerchief, but Cromwell forestalls me and hands me his own before taking the liberty of sitting down beside me.

"It is clean, Your Majesty."

I wipe away a tear, but another follows, and then another; great wet tears such as an infant weeps. Another sob, and my chest is so unbearably tight I fear I am going to suffocate.

"Oh Cromwell, what shall I do without her?"

His hand creeps out and, breaking all convention, he grasps my sleeve.

"The pain will pass, Your Majesty. It always does and then you will be able to contemplate the good memories of the times she spent with you. Memories are comforting, Sire. It is important not to push them aside. They help us cope in times of great stress."

It is the longest sentence I have ever heard him speak.

"But what shall I do now? How will I get through the rest of the day, the rest of the week?"

The rest of my life?

He stands up.

"Day by day, Your Majesty. Day by day. I shall escort you back to your apartments via your privy garden and inform the court you are indisposed. I will pass on the news on your behalf, if you will allow, and begin to make the arrangements. She will require a funeral fit for …"

"For a queen ..." My voice breaks. I wipe my cheeks again, sob again into Cromwell's fine linen kerchief.

"And you, Your Majesty, must stay in your chamber. My advice is to weep if you need to, for as long as you need to. It is the only way."

I take his arm and he walks me through my privy garden as if I am an old man, and he is my nurse.

July 1533

I should have listened when she pleaded sickness. I should have known Mary would never lie. As much as she hated Anne, she loved me. We were part of one another; without her I am broken, a cart with a damaged wheel, a horse with a snapped tendon. I will limp on through life without her, but I will never be the same.

As always, I keep the depth of my injury to myself. It will never do to have the people think me weak. I scribble a note of condolence to Brandon and order no expense spared for my sister's internment. For three weeks, candles burn day and night as she lies in state at Westhorpe. At Westminster, a requiem mass is held and the court fills with delegates come from France to join us in honouring their late queen. The last time England witnessed a funeral this lavish was for my grandmother, Margaret Beaufort, and that was long ago.

I sit alone in my palace and wonder if Mary is with Grandmother. Perhaps they are both looking down from Heaven at the splendour of the funeral I have arranged. I wonder if it pleases them.

They place her coffin on a velvet-draped hearse: 'The will of God is sufficient for me' emblazoned above her arms. I smile at the memory of her chosen motto. It always made me laugh for Mary was never one to accept anyone's will above her own ... not even God's.

I saw her effigy a few days ago; the wooden face devoid of life, like Mary yet quite unlike the Mary I knew. They dress it in her robes of state, a golden crown and sceptre to mark her queenly status. Six horses caparisoned in black are to draw her coffin, which will be surrounded by standard-bearers with the arms of Tudor and Brandon, and the Knights of Suffolk are to carry the canopy.

Leading the way, a hundred men with torches, then the clergy carrying the rood. Mary's staff will follow and, following the hearse, knights and nobles and yeomen. Behind them, Mary's daughter, Frances, and the ladies of her household, her friends and relatives, with parishioners taking up the rear. It will be a huge procession … as she deserves.

As she is laid to rest at the abbey of Bury St. Edmunds, the only two men who are not present are the two who loved her most. Henry Brandon, her husband, and Henry Tudor; her brother and king. It is a close and cloudy day, as if the sun is also mourning her loss. I don't want to see anyone – even Anne, so I closet myself away at Westminster while Brandon, no doubt, weeps alone at Westhorpe.

The world is emptier now and I am sad. Now she has gone there is no one who will dare mock me or remind me to be kind. I will never hear her high derisive laughter, or cringe at her jokes. I even miss her sly digs, those small comments that nobody but I knew were casting scorn on my kingly status. I miss her as badly as I would miss a limb.

I close my eyes, treading a lonely path back through the years to that day, before it all began, when we evaded our nurses to play in the meadow. I remember the high blue sky, the white buoyant clouds that changed before our eyes into wondrous things.

She was about five or six, and I was ten or eleven. We thought we had forever. We imagined our lives would be unchanging. The memory shines out like a beacon; my sister and I, Mary and me, clothed in innocence, unblemished, and pure.

Looking back, I recall that this was the day we learned of Arthur's death. I can see now that it was the very day my life began to crumble. Ever since then I've been trying to scramble back along the path to become that boy again, or at least to feel as carefree. With Mary in my life, I could sometimes forget how things have changed but now she has gone, the way back is somehow barred. I can only go forward, and I must do so alone.

August 1533

The corridor leading to the queen's apartments is crowded with people seeking audience. I am surprised she has more petitioners than me. Those who have been fortunate have managed to secure a window seat; the less fortunate are forced to stand. When I turn the corner, I encounter such a hubbub of voices that I am forced to pause, taking note of who waits upon her, and who is absent.

"Make way, the king is coming!" My page's shrill voice parts the crowd as surely as Moses parted the Red Sea. The conversation ceases, courtiers bow low as I pass by, and the massive doors are thrown open at my approach.

As I make to enter, I notice a dark-clad fellow, the next to be admitted to the queen's presence. I pause.

"Cromwell! There you are. I see the queen is keeping you waiting also."

He bows his head.

"Yes, Your Majesty, but it is no trouble to wait. I have little else to do."

I do not miss the irony. Since stepping from Wolsey's shadow, Thomas Cromwell has been busy indeed. The nobles sneer that there is nobody in the realm with their fingers in more pies than Cromwell. I favour him, despite the resentment of my council who sneer at his humble beginnings. I was still a young man when I learned from Wolsey that good breeding in a servant is not necessarily conducive to good service.

"Been waiting long?"

He smiles wryly.

"Oh, no, no. An hour or two at most, Your Majesty."

He bows his head.

"I will remind her you are here. She is no doubt engaged in baby talk or planning another masque. I will ... inform her."

He bows his head again and I pass into the chamber, the doors closing quietly behind me.

Inside the chamber is as noisy as the corridor. My arrival goes unnoticed until Purkoy leaps up and comes running, barking and growling in uncertain welcome.

I look down.

"And who do you think you are barking at, you silly little thing?" I scoop him up, cradle him in my elbow and smooth his coat.

He bridles with indignity.

"Henry!" Anne acknowledges my presence at last. I hand her the dog, which turns circles on her velvet skirt before settling. She smoothes the hair on his skull, and I swear his smile is one of ecstasy, his tongue lolling with pleasure. He winks at me smugly while Anne ruffles his fur.

"Did you bark at your papa, you naughty little man?" she says in a silly voice. "That isn't nice."

She pats the seat, inviting me to sit beside her, and I do her bidding.

"I am not his papa," I say quietly into her ear, and she throws back her head, laughing blithely at my discomfort.

"Well, I am his 'mama' so you must be. Besides, he looks just like you!"

She forces his head toward me, and I take note of the red fur, the wet black nose, the lovelorn eyes. I decide to let the matter drop.

"I expected you to be outside on the terrace. The day is fine. Were you not so …" I look down at her belly, "far advanced, I'd suggest a ride in the park."

She places both hands on the velvet dome that protects my son. "I doubt I would be able to mount even the smallest pony, Henry, but it won't be long now until the child is born. I shall be fit to hunt with you all winter. I dearly miss the chase and it seems so long since I was in the saddle."

More to the point, once my son is born, she will be back in my bed. I miss her presence there more than I ever did Kate's, perhaps because this time I have not looked for, or taken comfort elsewhere. The thought of coupling tightens my balls and I shift in the seat.

"You've been keeping secrets from me, Henry."

She looks at me askance and I cannot be sure if she is teasing. I stutter a reply while searching my mind for something I've failed to share with her.

"My brother, in his latest letter, suggested I try out one of your musicians. I took his advice, and he was right. This fellow should never have been kept away from me."

"What? Which fellow?"

"This one."

She waves a hand and her ladies part obligingly to reveal a young musician in their midst. He blushes when he realises he is the centre of our attention. Stumbling to his feet, he tugs at the hem of his doublet and clutches tighter to his lute.

"Smeaton, isn't it? I didn't keep him secret. He plays often at court."

"Well, I have never noticed him before. Come, Mark, play us another tune. He plays so well, Henry, I may keep him permanently in the corner to brighten my days."

"As if your days need brightening." I kiss her fingers and she endows me with her best smile.

Mark puts his foot on a stool and begins to sing, a dainty tune to please the ladies. They form a half-circle around him, hands clasped, their farthingales swinging like bells in time with his refrain. Smeaton warms to the adoration; his confidence increasing as his smile widens and his tune grows merrier.

Of course, they would admire him. He is young, no more than twenty, a youthful figure with dark curling hair, suggestive eyes. A boy, really, not a man. He makes me feel old and, suddenly, I feel jaded, and remind myself that I am yet in my prime. Smeaton is gauche.

"Dance, dance if you want to," Anne announces. "I cannot partake myself, but the king and I like to watch."

Norris bows before Nan Shelton and she takes his hand and follows him onto the floor. Soon, the chamber is alive with gaiety, swirling skirts, jingling jewellery, and leaping gentlemen. At my side, Anne claps gaily in time. I watch her, as deep in love with my queen as I was when she was Kate's lady-in-waiting. She was worth the wait, the frustration, the fury of the break from Rome.

I am blessed.

An hour or more passes before I remember Cromwell. I look up, remorseful at my forgetfulness.

"I forgot to say, Anne. Master Cromwell is waiting on you. I should have said sooner."

"Is he? I wondered why I'd not seen him today."

"You see him often?"

"Oh yes, about one thing and another. He champions many charities and begs me to do the same. Shall we see him now and spoil our fun, or shall I tell him to come back tomorrow? I could dismiss my women."

She wrinkles her brow, clearly reluctant to break up the joyful company. She is as pretty as blossom, her cheeks plumper than usual and she has more colour. Her breasts are ripe with childbirth, her bodice laced loosely to accommodate the child. I slide along the seat, our bodies close as I whisper into her ear.

"Dismiss the women but tell Cromwell to return tomorrow. I would be alone with my wife."

She looks up, eyes wide.

"But … you know I should not …"

"Yes, I know. I will bear that in mind."

The women do not hide their dismay at the spoiled party but obediently collect their instruments. Nan Shelton scoops a protesting Purkoy from the settle. As they depart, I hear them teasing Smeaton, his hesitant voice protesting. The door closes and we are alone.

"I never seem to see you alone these days," I complain, lifting her hand to my lips, turning it over and kissing her palm. I do not wait for her reply but fasten my mouth on hers, the remembered scent of her skin rousing me further.

"Come, come with me."

Reluctantly she allows me to lead her into her inner chamber, where I click my fingers and send her servants scurrying away. She sits on the edge of her bed and smiles uncertainly.

"My confinement will be soon," she says. "It's not too long to wait now."

"I know but … I miss you so much. If I could just …"

I begin to unfasten the front of her gown, push it from her shoulders and admire the way her skin glows beneath the sheer fabric of her shift. Her nipples are dark and her breasts are larger; they lie heavy in my palm, her belly resting in her lap. Tugging at the lacing, I pull the garment open, let it fall to her waist, and take a large brown nipple into my mouth, relishing the sweet moisture on my tongue.

Nourishment for my son.

My hands slip to her belly. I fall to my knees, softly stroke and kiss her taut skin, making her gasp and wriggle. My codpiece strains. I stand and shrug out of my doublet, letting it fall to the floor as I hoist her up the bed. She pulls up her skirts, obediently opening her knees. I want her. I need her. And her need matches mine, her eyes are dark, her mouth is slack with longing. But there is also terror. I know she will not refuse me but … I pause, bite my lip as anguish quilts her brow.

"I want to, Henry," she gasps. "I want to so much but … the child." She cradles her belly. "We should put the welfare of our prince before our passion."

She is right. Her sensible words fill me with shame. Slowly and painfully, I draw away.

"I am sorry, Anne. I – I … forgive me."

I fumble to retie my codpiece, let my fingers trail down her cheek before I stumble in agony from the chamber. As I close the door, I hear Anne groan and throw herself onto the mattress.

I wait for a moment, trying to regain my composure. My eyes are closed. The blood thumping in my veins fills my ears so I am both deaf and blind. I stumble further into the empty chamber and groan aloud.

"Your Majesty?"

A woman, Mary, I think, or Marge, stands before me, startled by my sudden presence. "Are you ill, Sire?"

I put a hand to my head, blood hammers against my skull.

"Are you well, Your Majesty? You look quite …"

She is young, bonny. I take a few steps toward her, grab her wrist and push her to an alcove. She does not resist. I am king. I loosen my codpiece again, lift her skirts, fight my way through a barrage of petticoats and … break faith with my wife.

It doesn't take long. Within minutes, I am straightening my clothes, offering her the use of my kerchief and begging forgiveness.

"I – I … Thank you, mistress. I will see … you shall not suffer for this if you do not speak of it."

Her eyes are huge, shining with … something. Shamed, I turn and flee, leaving her to compose herself as best she can. As I hurry back to my own apartment, I wave aside the greetings of courtiers and privy councillors and make straight for my private chapel to make confession and vent my shame.

It is quite late the next day before I can bring myself to visit Anne again. I have spent the morning and most of the afternoon wrestling with guilt, and the fear that the queen will discover my lack of faith.

When I promised before God to keep myself only unto Anne, it seemed such an easy promise to make. I was so sure that I would never return to the concubines I engaged while I was with Kate. I remained chaste for Anne's sake for seven, or maybe more, years while she refused to yield to me but, now we are wed, now I have had her … I cannot do without her.

In the days that follow, I visit the queen as little as I can while I make private penance. I deny myself my favourite food; I do not listen to my favourite music, nor ride out on the

24

hunt. For a while, I turn away from courtly life and spend my time in prayer, in penitence. The court whispers of my piety, the endearing manner in which the king prays for the queen's safe deliverance … and I do pray for those things, but I also pray for the strength to withstand bodily torment.

God knows, Anne must soon bring forth my heir.

Once Anne journeys to Richmond for her lying-in, the court seems very quiet. I have grown used to the sounds of laughter, the strains of music that floats from her adjoining apartment into mine. As the summer offers up one last burst of warmth, I am restless, at a loose end without my anchor, my Anne.

The morning sun streams through the window, sending mullioned shadows across the table. I reread the letter from my son, Henry Fitzroi, who has been in France for almost a year now.

He is soon to return to England to prepare for his marriage to Mary Howard. He writes carefully, but I notice that despite the maturity of the content, his hand still shows the mark of childhood although he has passed his fourteenth birthday.

I let the letter fall to the table.

It seems only yesterday that I rode in stealth to visit with Bessie after his birth. I recall unwrapping his bands, checking his limbs were straight, counting his fingers and toes. He pissed on me, as I recall. I remember Bessie's shocked face, fearful I would be angered by it, her relief when I laughed.

It seems like yesterday, yet that child has now almost reached manhood. It is not long ago that I considered making him my heir, but now I am to have a legitimate son, I still wish to honour Fitzroi. The boy that Anne bears will need supporters, strong family connections to safeguard his path to the throne. I must ensure his brother, and his sisters too, are part of that support. A union with the mighty Howard family will be good for both my sons.

Laughter floats up from the gardens, drawing me from the matter in hand. I look from the window where one of my household has grabbed his sweetheart and is seeking a kiss. He has her by the waist; she struggles ineffectively, giggles and glances up at the open window. Although I know she cannot see me, I draw back.

"Stop it," she says. "Someone may see us; the king may see us."

"He will understand. He knows how it feels to yearn for a woman as I do you."

She opens her mouth to protest further but he pulls her closer, silences her with kisses. I turn away. Jealous. I wish Anne were here that I might kiss her. I slump at the table and sigh so gustily the papers lift and shift.

"Is all well, Your Majesty?"

I look up to find Cromwell at my elbow.

"Oh, yes. Cromwell, you move so quietly. Nothing is amiss. I am just anxious for the child to be born. My son, Fitzroi, is also preparing to return to court. Today, I am lonely and lacking sons, but very soon I shall have two."

"Indeed, Your Majesty. The time will pass quickly. The wedding is to take place in November, I believe."

"Yes. He seems resigned to it rather than eager, but he is young yet. I am loath for the marriage to be consummated too early … you are aware of the circumstances surrounding my brother's death. Although the dowager princess denies it is so, it is very likely that the consummation of her marriage to Arthur weakened his constitution and led to his premature death."

"A sad consequence, Your Majesty, yet had he survived …"

"… had he survived, I'd be merely the Duke of York and Catherine would be queen. I dare say she has come to rue his death more than ever."

Uncertain how to answer, Cromwell bows his head and offers me a sheaf of papers.

"The arrangements for the announcements of the prince's birth, Your Majesty. I have had a draft made up …

should I leave enough room for amendment should the child … not be male?"

I look up, startled.

"Not be male? No, there is no need. Anne has promised me a son; the prophets have foreseen a son. There is no need for negativity."

He gathers the papers up again.

"Will that be all, Your Majesty?"

"For now. I might take a stroll outside."

As he prepares to leave, another question springs into my mind, born of loneliness.

"What news is there of Suffolk? I have missed his companionship these last months."

In truth, I've missed the ease of our friendship since I took up with Anne. In her final years, Suffolk and my sister kept away from court, their dislike for Anne outweighing their love for me. Now Mary that is gone, and Brandon is widowed, I had hoped he'd return … permanently.

Cromwell clears his throat.

"As I understand it, the duke is up to his neck in debt, missing your late sister's dower payments from France, no doubt."

"Yes. I have already waived a substantial portion of his debt to the Crown and bestowed upon him the see of Ely – no small thing. But he enjoys a lavish lifestyle and has two small boys to raise and numerous wards to care for. We must consider what further measures may be taken to help him."

Cromwell bows and when I do not speak again, he leaves me. I must write to Anne before I take my walk in the garden. I call for a fresh pen and paper. A servant brings it, turns to leave.

"Have the dogs made ready for a walk," I say. "I will be ready for them in half an hour or so."

It is hot. I take a kerchief and mop my brow, replace my hat.

"Are you too warm, Your Majesty? Do you wish to retire to the hall?"

27

"No, no. I wish to walk."

The attendant falls back with the others. I look about the calming garden where the scent of summer is heavy in the air. I have walked this path since I was knee high, following in the wake of Grandmother, hand in hand with Mary. Very little has changed; the honey-coloured gravel still crunches beneath my feet, the lavender still infuses the air I breathe. If I were brought here blindfold, I would know by the sounds and the fragrance just where I am in the world. The only difference is, I am alone now.

All those people with whom I walked here are gone. Grandmother, my mother, my sister, and even Kate is living far away, hating me no doubt. And Brandon, who could be here, but is not.

I am not alone, of course, not as other people might be. My every footstep is dogged by servants, courtiers, and Cut and Ball and Beau, replacements of my childhood friends, are over there, tails waving as they investigate the foot of the hedge. But it isn't the same. I miss my companions of old, the certainty of those days, the security of being a princeling instead of king of it all.

"Your Majesty?"

The voice breaks into my gloomy musing. I look up, take three steps toward the speaker.

"Brandon? By God, man, my thoughts must have conjured you!"

He laughs, a shadow of his old grin, and I notice how much thinner his face is, and the strands of grey that now lace his beard. I take his hand, pat his shoulder, blink away an unmanly tear.

"I hope I find you well, Sire."

Silence falls briefly. I shake my head.

"Well in body, Brandon, but low of spirit. I expect you are the same."

"I have been low, yes, and dogged by problems as you know. But we should look to the future. You will feel better once the queen is back to cheer you. We will all feel better ..."

He stares bleakly across the garden, the knowledge that his own queen will never return to cheer him loud between us.

"It will ease, you know, Brandon; the pain, I mean. We will one day look back on her life and laugh and feel blessed."

"I already feel blessed, Your Majesty ..."

"'*Your Majesty?* What is all this? Why am I no longer 'Hal'?"

"Hal," he smiles sheepishly. "I was trying to work my way to begging a boon of you, Sire."

I hope it isn't money he wants. We walk a few paces along the path, his hands clasped behind his back, head down.

"Well? Surely you aren't afraid to ask."

"Not afraid, no, but wary of giving offence."

"Take your chance, man. I am waiting."

He looks up at the sky, squints at the brightness, moistens his lips.

"You know I loved your sister; she was, as they say, the love of my life."

"I am aware of that, Brandon. You risked enough to win her."

He looks into my eyes, laughter dancing with regret and sorrow.

"They were such days, Hal ... such days."

"Yes."

We walk on in silence while he composes his request.

"Days like that will never come again. I loved Mary more than I can ever love another, yet ... her passing has left me in dire need."

He wrings his hands and the irony of a man clad in silk and velvet and hung with gold pleading need does not escape me. Yet I do not remark on it. "The thing is, Your Majesty ... Hal. I have the mind to marry again."

"Marry? But it is less than ..."

"Three months; yes, I know, but I have children to feed, a household to maintain. If I am to keep ..."

"Whom do you wish to wed?"

29

"Katherine Willoughby." He winces, does not meet my eye.

"Willoughby? Your ward? Is she not ... young?"

"I can guarantee she will grow older, Sire."

"Forgive me, is she not affianced to your son?"

"But he is only ten; he cannot wed her for four years at least."

"And she is what ... fourteen, to your fifty years."

"I have six more months until I reach fifty; pray Sire, do not age me."

A flash of his old humour. I laugh but I am not altogether happy.

"Have you spoken to her? Is there a need for you to wed? Was there something between you while ... before ...?"

"NO, never, I swear it!"

I believe him. I have to.

"If the lady is agreeable, then I see no bar to it, but people will talk, you know that."

"People will talk whether I remarry or not. I am confident Katherine will welcome the marriage. I suspect she would prefer to marry me than a ten-year-old boy."

Katherine must be no more than fourteen, the age gap between her and Brandon far greater than between her and the boy. We both know Brandon craves the inheritance of her Willoughby estates more than the pleasure of her untouched body, but neither of us speaks of it.

"And what does your son think?"

"I can only guess, but as yet he has little liking for girls, so I expect him to make no loud protest."

I throw back my head, the bellow of laughter bringing the attention of the courtiers who follow in our wake. I wave them back and, placing my hand on Brandon's shoulder, we move slowly through the garden, passing into the welcome shade of a sprawling pear tree. Brandon removes his cap and uses it to bat away a late, lazy wasp.

"I hope you will be at court more often once you are married, Brandon."

He puts up a hand to cover mine. "I hope so too, Your Majesty."

7th September 1533 – Greenwich

The day is here, less than two weeks since the queen took to her lying-in chamber. I have barely finished dressing and am still surrounded by gentlemen when a messenger arrives with news that the queen's pains have begun. I snatch the letter he carries and scan the words, before looking up from the parchment.

"Gentlemen," I say, as my heart swells. "Today is a great day, for today we shall see the arrival of our prince."

A ripple of cheer eddies around the room. "Come, come, hurry up and lace my sleeves and order up the barge. I will journey to Greenwich to be on hand when the boy is born."

It is several hours before I have broken my fast and attended a hasty Mass, and the sun has passed its zenith before I make my way to the waiting barge. It is not an official trip so there is no great ceremony as the oarsmen push off and head up the river to Greenwich.

As we glide across the deep green water, I lie back in my seat and ponder on whether to call my son Henry or Edward.

The question of his name has been on my mind since long before his conception. I would love to call him Henry, for it would mean that when … I am gone, England would be ruled by King Henry IX and ensure that each time his name is spoken my own will be conjured, ensuring that I too am remembered. But although Fitzroi will never be king, he already bears that name.

Anne frowns each time the matter is raised, complaining that it was rash of me to name Fitzroi in my own honour.

"It would be ridiculous to use the name again; bestowing it on a bastard has robbed it of value. I suppose it will have to be Edward."

Edward, after my grandfather. I tend to agree. It is a nod toward the legitimacy of my Plantagenet forebears and moves away from the question of the disputed legitimacy of the maternal Beaufort line, on which my father based his claim.

Edward, my son, come here!

Silently, I practise speaking to him; imagine his eyes that will be as blue as mine, his hair that will be as red, his limbs that will be both strong and fine. I will teach him everything a king needs to know, so he will ascend to the throne fully educated in kingship and more confident than I ever was. The boy Anne is shortly to bear me will be a king such as England has never seen.

I raise my chin, smiling across the stretch of Thames where a trio of swans flies low across the water. They grunt with each flap of their wings, as if too old for the effort. As they disappear from view, a sudden breeze sets the curtains flapping and the pennants on the stern snap as if struggling for freedom. The barge follows the bend of the river and I draw my cloak about my shoulders, suppressing a shiver as the palace of Greenwich comes into view.

This was my mother's favourite palace, the place where my siblings and I were born. Close by is Eltham where we were raised, the nursery where Margaret, Mary and I were happy until the day we learned of Arthur's death.

The sight of it brings back memories of infant mischief; Mary's infectious laughter, the games we played, the nurses that despaired of us. Sadness, a longing for those days, settles briefly on my shoulders, but I shake it off.

This is a day of joy, a time of celebration. A day to look ahead.

Today, a future king of England will be born.

We glide toward the bank. When the oarsmen put up their oars, droplets of river water fall like silver rain as we bump against the wharf. My servants leap ashore first and stand ready to assist should I require their aid, but I brush them off, stride confidently along the gangplank and once on *terra firma* look up at the palace windows.

Somewhere, deep in the heart of this beloved building, my wife, my queen – my precious Anne – struggles to bring forth my son and heir.

I am not worried for her safety or for the well-being of my son because God is on my side. I have put an end to my illegal union with Kate and, in reward, Anne and I are shortly to be blessed. God will ensure that nothing goes amiss, and Anne is safely delivered of my son.

I sprint up the steps to the hall and pause to throw off my cloak. As I mount the stairs, two at a time, I draw off my gloves and unbuckle my sword. At the top, the guards snap to attention.

"How is the queen?" I ask the first woman I encounter. "Her labours are progressing well?"

"So I believe, Your Majesty."

She does not meet my eye but sinks into a deep curtsey. I pass on, into a parlour where a servant pours and offers me refreshment. Cup in hand, I walk to the window, looking out across the garden to the river stretching its green, serpentine body toward London, which glints in the distance like a star on the edge of the world.

I turn.

"Has anyone sent for news of the queen? Do I have to go to her myself?"

While they scurry away to do my bidding, I stride the length of the room, pausing at the wall where twin portraits of my mother and father hang. Their faces are stiff, eyes staring, yet they are recognisable. If only Mother were here. She would be proud of me this day, and even Father, who in life never let me glimpse an iota of paternal pride, would admit that I have done well.

I examine his portrait but see nothing of myself in his thin features, his dispassionate eyes.

Look at me now, Father. I am king. I have a fertile wife, and the birth of my heir is imminent. I have followed your instruction. *I have not failed.*

I sense the long line of my ancestors looking down on me with approval. I imagine them raising their heavenly glasses; *Good for you, Henry*, they seem to say. *You have done well.*

I turn at the sound of a footstep, an expectant smile I cannot erase teasing my lips upwards, my heart racing a little faster.

"Well?"

The servant licks his lips, his eyes slide away to the far corner.

"Well? What news have you? Has my son been born?"

"The – the queen has been delivered, Your Majesty; the child was born at close to three of the clock."

Delight stabs my heart. I step eagerly forward to grasp the boy by the shoulders.

"And he is well? Is the boy healthy?"

The servant swallows, fear in his face, a man facing demons. The first stirring of doubt dulls my joy. He wets his lips and I see his Adam's apple bouncing in his throat as he seeks to locate his voice.

"Sh-she is, Your Majesty, as far as we can tell."

Like a great fallen bell, optimism crashes to my feet, tolling the end of my hopes. Another moment follows during which I cannot speak, can barely breathe. My mind whirls.

"What?"

I speak quietly through tight lips before I realise I have taken hold of his shoulders. Instantly, I release him and the servant cringes away, clasps his hands, his shoulders hunched.

"The - the queen was delivered of a healthy girl, Your Majesty. I – I had the news directly from one of her women."

I turn away and move back to the window, looking out at the garden again. The sun has gone in now; the colours of the meadow and flowers that a few moments ago were vibrant are now muted and grey, like my heart.

I close my eyes; feel the trickle of a tear as my throat tightens. I swipe the moisture away, but another tear gathers.

A footstep.

"Your Majesty?"

It is Norfolk's voice.

34

"Get out."

I do not turn. I will not give them the satisfaction of seeing me weep like a broken boy over the birth of another daughter. Retreating footsteps, a slamming door and then … silence.

I slump onto the window seat.

A girl, a useless girl. I sink my head into my hands. *What have I done to deserve this? Why does God turn his back on me when all I do is strive to serve my country in His name?* These past seven years I have wept, fought, imperilled my kingdom, and torn the country apart that I might divorce Kate and make Anne my legitimate queen. I placed my very soul in peril by breaking with Rome and what is the reward for all my suffering?

Another worthless princess.

I am afraid to face her, yet I must. The corridors leading to Anne's chambers seem vast, stretching to eternity. The faces that line my path seem to melt, sliding from view as they sink into obeisance, but I make no acknowledgement. The door looms suddenly, large and dark, but is quickly thrown open at my approach.

On the threshold, I hesitate. If I could only turn and flee. If only I could re-throw the dice, go back to this morning when there was hope and happiness, and joy in the future. Optimism. Oh, what I would give for another chance, another outcome, a different future.

I've faced this too many times before with Kate and I have no will to do so again. I cannot go back. I am caught in a trap, snared by barren women who refuse to bear me a son.

"Your Majesty."

The voice jerks me from the daze and before I know it, I have passed into the lying-in chamber. Women are dotted about the room; they rise and curtsey at my entrance, but no one dares speak. They await my cue, but I lack the words to make this right. At length, one of them, braver than the rest, moves forward to stand before me, a mouse-like creature in a blur of blue silk, pale and meek. I look into her pitying eyes.

"The queen is awake, Your Majesty. She wondered if you might come."

I shouldn't be here, of course. The lying-in chamber is no place for a man, but I am not just any man. I am king … who has the power to stop me?

But now I am here on the threshold of the birthing chamber, I wish to God I'd stayed away.

Quietly, the woman ushers me to the inner chamber door. It opens slowly, revealing darkness, muted light, a roaring fire. I pass like a dreamer into the presence of my wife.

"Henr-"

Anne's voice breaks. I see a hag, white skin, hollow eyes; a hag that opens her arms. I wearily find the resolve to drag my eyes to look at her properly. Her face is paler than her bed linen, her eyes huge and black, her nose red and moist from weeping, and there is a streak of blood on her forehead.

There is nothing in the least alluring about her now.

She opens her arms wider, demanding that I fill them, but I do not go to her. I cannot. Slowly, I turn my head to where a woman is bending over the royal cradle, the screeching child within protesting at the change of swaddling.

"Leave us."

The woman turns, open-mouthed, and waves her arm toward the cradle.

"But Your Majesty, the child is …"

"I said, 'leave us.'"

She makes a hasty curtsey before fleeing our presence. With an anguished wail, Anne dives beneath the covers, blessedly muffling her noisy grief. My limbs are as heavy as my heart as I force myself toward the hearth and peer over the side of the cradle.

The child is naked and livid with rage. Her flesh, still smeared with birth fluid, is wrinkled. I observe the red face, the red hair, the flailing limbs, the bloody stump of the cord that once bound her to her mother. This should have been my prince … my heir, but she has no prick – she is a useless girl.

Grief closes like grasping hands about my throat, robbing me of breath. *What am I to do with another daughter?*

Her thrashing limbs are rigid, her toes flexed, her furious fists battling the unknown world into which she has been so rudely thrust. I know how she feels. I want to scream too.

How the kings of Europe will laugh when they hear of this.

I lean closer, noting the transparency of her skin, the blue veins on her temple, the tiny chin that judders with the injustice of her life.

I can relate to that. I reach into the cradle, offer her a finger and she grabs it readily, quieting a little, her chest heaving as she blinks and frowns in an effort to focus. My heart calms. She is mine, at least – there is no doubt that she shares my Tudor lineage.

There is no doubt about that at all.

I scoop the raging scrap of femininity into my arms and settle her in the crook of my elbow before glancing toward the bed where Anne clings to the refuge of her covers.

Strands of her hair trail blackly across her pillow. This is not how a queen should behave. It might only be a girl but at least her child is living, breathing. Kate showed more courage than this even when our children were born dead.

"Stop this."

The bed-ropes sink beneath my weight as the child ceases to cry, her gums hard and insistent on my knuckle.

"Anne, come, the child is in need of suckling."

After a moment, the blankets heave and Anne's tear-streaked face emerges from beneath. She slides up the pillow, wincing, I presume, at the tenderness of her nethers. I smile but it is tight and forced, my heart is not in it.

This is all Anne's fault.

She promised me a son.

She lied to me.

I should rage at her, but I shake off the anger. It will not serve me now. I will nurture it.

"My mother nursed us herself for the first few weeks," I say. "It is not the usual custom for royalty, but I suppose you intend to do the same."

She makes no answer but wipes her cheeks on her nightgown and attempts to present a cheery face.

"I will do as you think best, Henry," she says, surprising me with the meekness of her tone. I lean forward, offer her the child, and she takes her from me as if she's been handling infants all her life.

She sinks back on the pillows, loosens the neck of her gown and offers her daughter the teat. The small breasts I used to love are swollen and blue-veined, the nipple fat and brown. I watch my wife and daughter together, the slurping noises of the greedy child almost bringing a smile. The appetites of a Tudor prince are embodied in the form of a girl.

Tentatively, Anne takes her eyes from the infant and looks at me. She presents a horrid sight; straggled hair, red-rimmed eyes, gaunt cheeks. There is not a scrap remaining of the vibrant, sophisticated woman I fell in love with.

"I am so sorry, Henry. I never dreamed this would happen. I was so certain …"

Her mouth goes out of shape and her throat works while she struggles to speak.

I look away.

Life repeats itself. I had believed that once I was rid of Kate, and married to Anne, God would favour me with sons. *What does this mean?* Is it a sign of His disfavour? Is it a test? Some Heavenly jape?

But God doesn't play games, and He doesn't offer clues to life's puzzles.

So, what must I do? I know beyond doubt that I am supposed to get an heir, but how far must I go to get one, and what further sacrifices must I make to secure the Tudor line?

I blink at the Marian scene before me. My wife and daughter present a pretty picture; all it requires is a male child to perfect it. How different everything would be. What joy would befall the nation.

Anne leans forward, anoints the baby's forehead with her lips, the curtain of dark hair falling forward.

I sigh, close my eyes, and concede defeat.

"Well, it is done now. In the circumstances we can scarcely name her Henry or Edward – I was wondering … what you think of the name Elizabeth?"

Her head jerks up, and she beams over our daughter's head into my eyes. A shade of the old Anne; the woman who stole my heart and my senses, the woman I turned the realm upside down to possess.

"After my mother, Henry? Oh yes, Elizabeth is the perfect name."

I envy her swiftly returning joy, her eternal optimism that tomorrow will provide us with all we desire. She has not yet become as jaded as me. I join them on the bed and forbear to remind her that Elizabeth was also my mother's name.

I cancel the jousts and banquets organised to welcome my son into the world, but the christening will go ahead as planned. It is to be the greatest ever seen. Even though the queen and I will not be attending, I insist on the best of everything. Nobody in the kingdom must be allowed to guess at our disappointment that our first-born child is not a boy. There will be other children; there is plenty of time for Anne to bear me a son yet.

I am in my prime, and Anne is not yet too old. And daughters can be useful. When the time comes, I will secure a good match for her, with France perhaps to antagonise Spain.

Kate will hate that.

The route from the Great Hall to the Church of the Observant Friars is marked by a thick carpet of rushes, and rich tapestries are hung along the way. Further hangings are placed in the church to screen Elizabeth from draughts. Her health must be preserved at all costs.

Everyone of note has been invited: foreign dignitaries; emissaries; and, from closer to home, the mayor and council, our friends and family. Even, at Anne's insistence, our enemies … *her* enemies.

Her eyes sparkle as she lists their names and imagines their discomfort at the ostentation with which we welcome our royal princess – our heir, until such time as her brother is born.

"Those that hate me will write at once to Catherine and tell her," Anne says. "I hope she sickens of the news."

Anne has not yet left confinement and is tired of bed. She complains that she wants to get up and dress, to re-enter court and take part in the plans for the festivities.

"I haven't yet had a chance to be a proper queen," she says. "I was too sickly while carrying Elizabeth to fully appreciate my role. There is so much to do, so much to plan. I cannot wait for my churching."

I lean forward in my seat.

"You need to focus on giving our child into the care of the wet nurse and returning to my bed. We've a prince to make, and it needs to be done quickly too."

She smiles suggestively, the lusty looks at odds with her plump, maternal cheeks but I know once she is separated from the child her former allure will return.

The christening party left for the abbey several hours ago and Anne is anxious for Elizabeth's return. Her breasts are full of nourishment and causing her discomfort. I have found it awkward to fill the waiting time with conversation; resentment for her failure is still so strong within me.

I am glad when voices in the corridor alert us to their return; Anne's sister, Mary, is the first to arrive. She bursts into the chamber, stopping short when she sees me. She sinks into a curtsey and when she rises, her flushed face betrays her embarrassment at our former intimacy; she remembers it each time we meet … as do I.

"What was it like, Mary?" Anne asks, holding out her arms for the princess. "Was Elizabeth good? Did she cry? Was she fretting for me?"

"She slept right through the ceremony. She barely stirred even when she was anointed with the holy oil," Mary replies as she turns away and folds the child's shawl. "Everyone was there. Mary of Norfolk bore the chrisom and the old duchess carried Elizabeth. She was swathed in royal purple and Father bore the train with Norfolk and Suffolk to either side."

"I know all that but what did people say? What did they do?"

Anne loosens her bed gown and, with little pig-like grunts of contentment, Elizabeth seeks the dug and begins to suckle. I make a note to myself to make sure a wet nurse is engaged without delay; the longer Anne nurses the child, the longer it will take to beget a prince. Mary bends over and rummages in a clothespress for clean linen for the child. At the thought of Anne's return to my bed, I surreptitiously ease my codpiece; although Marge continues to serve my needs during her lying-in, it is the queen I need. Only Anne can give me the son I crave.

1534 - 35

When Elizabeth is given a household of her own and departs court, the queen falls into gloom. She does her best to hide it, but the signs are unmistakeable; she is listless in bed and has no appetite at the table. I tempt her with sweetmeats; buy her a cage of birds and a jewelled necklet with a pearl the size of a quail's egg. She accepts everything with a watery smile but although she gets one of her women to fasten the jewel about her neck and makes little kissing sounds to the cage of finches, I am not fooled.

What she needs is another child.

I encourage her to immerse herself in the joys of court life, ordering pageants, arranging hunting parties. Her chambers begin to fill with new gowns, and she orders dozens of shoes and jewelled girdles. It is worth the cost just to have her smile again, but I cannot help but wonder where it will stop.

"How can you require so many shoes?" I exclaim with mock surprise. "You only have one pair of feet! There are enough here to shoe the entire court."

She turns up her face, mockery in her laugh that I'd despaired of hearing again.

41

"You can choose a pair, if you wish, Henry. These pink velvet ones should suit you."

I had never realised so many variations on a French hood were possible, or so many ways to wear a sleeve. But Anne isn't all about clothes. She has a keen mind, a sharp wit, and an acute grasp of politics. Once she grows used to the child's absence and I take her back into my bed, she quickly returns to her old self. When she isn't practising new dance steps, writing to Elizabeth's governess, or exchanging rhyming couplets with her friends, she seeks me out in my private apartment where the rest of the court cannot follow.

I am trying to compose a tune and scarcely listening to her prattle.

"Cromwell is right, Henry, the church is corrupt and in dire need of reform. It will be a simpler task to reconfigure things now we are free of the Pope."

I try out the verse in a different key.

"Henry, are you listening?"

"Of course, of course ... erm, what were you saying?"

She casts her eyes heavenward, thumps a pillow and repeats it.

"Indeed." I always feel a dart of fear when I am reminded of our excommunication from Rome, but I never allow it to show.

"Cromwell says the people have been fooled by tricks and mummery. He claims the phial of Christ's blood at Hailes Abbey is more than likely to be that of a duck, and ..."

Reluctantly, I put down my lute.

"We will investigate. I have already spoken to him about it; you don't have to repeat his every word."

She pouts, the frown darkening her features. Sometimes I feel she will never be content, although I go to great lengths to make her happy.

In January, an act was passed recognising the legality of our marriage and barring Mary from the succession. Until such time as a son is born to us, Elizabeth is now my only legal heir, yet still Anne is not satisfied. She meddles constantly in state affairs. Why can she not be content to be a wife and mother? Why is she not yet with child? Perhaps these serious matters are compromising her fertility. Her mind should be full of sweet things, flowers and sunshine. Matters of doctrine are for men to worry about.

"Come," I say, "put on a cheerful face and show me the dance steps you've been practising."

She frowns again.

"Life cannot just be about enjoyment, Henry. What about the other matter? Am I permitted to discuss that?"

It is my turn to frown.

"What other matter?"

She gives a small growl of anger, like my spaniels do when I have inadvertently stepped on a paw.

"The warrant, Henry, have you signed her death warrant?"

I had feared as much. Shuffling my papers, I prevaricate, putting off the moment for as long as I can.

"I thought to make her suffer a while longer. Sometimes the torments of confinement, together with the uncertainty of one's fate, offers greater suffering than the ultimate penalty."

"She must be quite mad. You know that."

The Mad Maid of Kent, as they've named her, has been a thorn in my flesh for some time now. At first, I tried to ignore her but her voice against me grew too loud. She railed publicly about my marriage to Anne, claiming Kate was the true queen and Mary my true heir. Cromwell has warned her, but nothing would still her tongue. Now she speaks against my rule and claims God no longer regards me as king of England. She has been taken to the Tower and is set for execution, but I am reluctant to take her head. Cromwell thinks, and I agree, that to do so would grant her the martyrdom she craves.

She is crazed, of course, but people harken to her ravings. Madness is always unsettling, terrifying, yet the more we try to muffle this woman, the louder she grows and if we silence her for good her voice will become all the louder.

"Well?" Anne snaps me from my reverie. I fiddle with the ring on my forefinger and make reply.

"Yes, you are right. She is entirely mad. Cromwell says she is central in a popish conspiracy against us. She will hang soon but not before she has witnessed the disembowelment of her fellow conspirators and seen them burn. She will be clear then on the punishment that awaits her. The punishment that awaits all traitors."

Anne's uncharacteristic silence forces me to turn to face her. She is standing by the window in a shaft of sunlight, her coif in her hands, her hair falling softly about her shoulders. Her eyes meet mine, her face is white, her mouth open, her eyes are dark with intent. She is so beautiful that something stirs in my nethers, and my need for her is so great I am constrained to move toward her.

She takes my hands, grasps them tightly and stares fiercely into my eyes.

"But when, Henry, when will she hang? It must be soon."

*

Anne laughs, digs in her heels, and urges her mount forward. Taken by surprise, I gallop in pursuit, duck beneath low hanging trees and splash through a ford. She rides swiftly, her mare less encumbered than mine. Every so often, delighted at having the better of me, she turns in the saddle to glance over her shoulder, her laughter trailing in her wake like the end notes of a song.

The ground speeds beneath us but since my horse is stronger and bigger, I swiftly catch up with her. When we are neck and neck, I reach out, grab the reins, and haul her horse to a halt. Conceding defeat, she pants from the exertion, her cheeks for once full of colour, her eyes wet from the wind. She pulls a stray strand of hair from her mouth.

"I would have beaten you fair and square, Henry. You cannot avoid the issue by stopping the race."

"I am your king. I can do as I wish."

I endeavour to make my voice stern, but she knows I am jesting and looks about the glade. My eyes follow hers and

44

absorb the beauty of the sunlight as it casts dappled golden light on to the woodland floor.

"It is pretty here," she says. "Shall we walk for a while?"

I dismount and hasten to help her from her horse before our attendants catch up with us. As she slides to the ground, I keep my hands about her waist, lean in for a kiss but she pulls away, casts a nod toward the blushing groom who has just trotted up.

"Not here, husband. Let us walk a little deeper into the wood."

On this bright morning, we could be anyone. I could be some lowly lord, and she the lady of my heart. We discard the cares of state, the trials of kingship, to revel in the treasures of the countryside.

I halt beneath the bole of a great oak and pull her close again. The aroma of her skin is equine, a mixture of horseflesh and hay, fresh air and grass. I pluck a few small leaves and twigs that have become caught in her hair during our wild ride.

"I could take you now, my lady."

She stiffens, returns my kiss but then she pulls away.

"Although I should love to accept such a tempting offer, Henry, I fear I must refuse."

"Refuse your king?"

I scowl, disgruntled at her refusal, but she merely laughs and tugs my beard.

"A few moments since you were playing at being not my king but merely some ardent landowner lusting after a country wife."

I give her a playful shake.

"And you are supposed to play along, not act the high and mighty - 'ooh, don't touch me, Sire.'"

She places a hand on my chest, fending off my kisses.

"But Henry, in the circumstances, it would perhaps not be wise."

"It is always wise to oblige your ... what do you mean, 'in the circumstances?'"

Her face is infused with delight. She can scarcely contain her news.

"I mean, Sir, that it is possible, although not absolutely certain, that I may be with child and would not wish to…"

"With child? You knew you were with child and yet rode like a hoyden through the wood? Have you no sense …" But then the reality of her words hits me, and relief and joy erase every other feeling. "Oh, Anne, Anne – a child, at last. This time, this time, you will give me my son."

Those words repeat in my mind - this time, this time it *will* be a son. I will visit with her every day, no longer a demanding lover but a concerned father-to-be. As difficult as it is to forego our marital pleasures, I must limit myself to a more platonic love.

I draw her close, kiss her ear, and stroke her cheek.

"You must take every precaution …"

"Of course, I will, Henry."

"No, I mean *every* precaution; no more hunting, no dancing, no … I will not bother you until he is safely born."

She throws back her head, her merry laugh mocking. I let go her hand.

"Then we will be many months apart, my lord. I have only just missed what I should have seen. Do you remember the torture of being apart before?"

I remember it. How can I forget watching her bloom and grow, becoming more beautiful and somehow more desirable in her unattainability? But I also remember the assignations with her woman and the service she provided in my time of need. She is still at court, which is fortunate, for I may have need of her again.

For a few weeks, I watch and wait but, as time passes and Anne shows no sign of miscarrying our child, I begin to make plans. I cannot help but imagine his face. Will he resemble me, or Anne? Elizabeth is a curious mix of both of us, her features keen and sharp like her mother's but her red hair and complexion are mine. I fancy a son in my own image, a big lusty lad whom I can mould into the sort of prince

England deserves. I will ensure he is unsurpassed in the tiltyard, and on the hunting field. We will wrestle together, hunt and play tennis. We will make fine music and he will be a boy after my own heart, made in my own image, and I shall name him …

That same question, the dilemma of choosing a king's name. I had a son named Henry before, a fine boy who lasted but a sennight. And my bastard, Fitzroi, he is called Henry, too. I must choose another name. Edward perhaps, after my grandfather … or Edmund after my maternal grandfather. Both were warriors but only one was a king.

I hear a noise beyond the chamber, and I am pulled from my musings by the arrival of Cromwell, who brings the inevitable business of kingship to occupy me for a time.

"We must discuss the matter of the mad nun," Cromwell says. "The longer we delay, the louder her voice, the bigger her …"

"Yes, yes, just see to it, would you. There is no other way. It is unfortunate we cannot dispense with her quietly, but she has too much support to get away with that. Is there much business to be dealt with today? I have asked Brandon to attend me. I am sending him to France to rearrange our proposed visit, since it seems the queen will be, erm … indisposed and unable to travel at that time."

He gathers up his papers, bows deeply and gratifyingly.

"I wish you a good day, Your Majesty, and I shall wait upon you again in the morning."

I accompany him to the door, my hand on his shoulder until I pause at the threshold and watch him walk away. As he goes, I note how unobtrusively he moves around the palace. Where his old master, Wolsey, went about with great pageantry, each and every arrival announced as if he were some great king, Cromwell is as quiet as a beetle in the wainscot.

It is late April when, still spitting vitriol against me, the mad nun finally goes to the scaffold. Once she is dispatched, the silence is blissful. I close my ears to those who mutter against the immorality of her death, but those whom I suspect offered her their silent support are now watched. Cromwell sets spies on them. Dissention against the crown will not be tolerated.

Preparations are underway for a new law that will soon be passed through parliament – an act that will name me as Head of the Church in England, and all men will be constrained to swear to it. As always, I am frustrated at the length of time it takes to organise such matters. It seems a simple enough change to make – we have already dispensed with the Pope, and it is fitting that I should take his place as God's representative on Earth. But the council, and Cromwell in particular, are keen that every detail is made watertight. Once the act has been passed, it will be treason to disavow the Act of Supremacy. I foresee no problems, for I have learned that with a little persuasion most men are agreeable to my wishes.

At times, I feel besieged from all sides. There is trouble in Ireland and, although that is not unusual, this latest rebellion is the last straw. I recall William Skeffington to be Lord Deputy of Ireland and send him off with orders to show no mercy, for I am determined that this uprising will be the last.

And as if I haven't enough problems, the Act of Supremacy that Cromwell assured me would be a simple matter is not progressing smoothly. Why can the people not see I do this *only* for the benefit of the country? I am simply replacing a despot, whose main objective is Rome, with their king, who has always placed the good of England before all else. What can they possibly see wrong with that?

In the taverns, people mutter against the Act, and traders argue about it in the marketplace. And as for the monks – gah, the religious community whose welfare is my primary concern – they shout the loudest of all. But I will remind them that I am their king, and they will either accept the change and deny the Bishop of Rome, or take the consequences.

I am at my desk, a burning candle illuminating the papers before me. To my left, the pile I have dealt with is small; to my right, the matters still outstanding teeter like the Tower of Babylon. From the next room, the voices of Anne and her companions filter to me, the occasional strain of music worming its way into my concentration and pulling me from my task. I sigh, and let my quill drop, a scattering of ink spots spoiling the cuff of my sleeve.

I close my eyes, squeeze the bridge of my nose, and concede that it is almost too dark to see. Snapping my fingers for a servant to refill my wine, I watch the thick red liquid pour into the cup and sit back in my chair. Glad to finally put off the trials of the day, I sigh again, but this time it is with contentment.

Someone enters. I squint into the gloom.

"Your Majesty, I hoped you could spare a few moments."

"Cromwell, come in, man, don't lurk in the doorway."

He moves forward, a clutch of parchment beneath his arm. "What is it, not more trouble from Ireland?"

"No, Your Majesty ... although that wouldn't entirely be a surprise to me. No, it is closer to home. The Order of Observant Friars ..."

"Greenwich?"

"Yes, Your Majesty. Despite our strong advice that they keep silent, they continue to speak out against the Act. I feel gentle persuasion has failed and more stringent methods should be ..."

I thump the desk.

"Then they leave us no choice. We will close them down. My tolerance is at an end, and I am done with them. Give the ringleaders a taste of the Tower and turn the others onto the street. We will take possession of their building and chattels."

"Your Majesty." Thomas bows in acquiescence. "Erm, you will broach the matter with the queen? I fear she will not be pleased."

"She will do my bidding, Cromwell. It isn't as if we haven't tried to settle the matter amicably."

"Perhaps if we were to set out guidance, a new canon law if you like, it would lay to rest the concerns of the monks."

It has not proved a simple matter to detail exactly which religious traditions will change, and which remain. I abhor the evangelicals who seem to see my reforms as a show of royal support for their beliefs. It is not the religion that must change but the methods of worship. Popes and monks are too much, there is no longer any need for them here in England where I am now God's representative. God and I need no interpreter.

From now on, I will be the one to stand between a man and his God. We have no need for the intervention of Rome. I frown. This business is giving me a headache. It is late in the day to be discussing such things. I want to join my wife's frolic, not sit in this gloomy chamber discussing business.

I drain my cup, slam it down on the desk.

"Tomorrow, Cromwell, we will continue this tomorrow."

He backs hastily away as I brush past him and through the door into Anne's company. The laughter and dancing stops, the music dwindles into discordance.

"Henry!"

Anne claps her hands and comes to greet me, drawing me into the centre of the room. "We are trying to fit Tom Wyatt's poem to music and not one of us can agree which refrain is best suited. You, my husband, must have the final say."

Tom Wyatt is overseas on a mission for the crown. Several years ago, deeming their close friendship neither healthy nor appropriate, I felt it necessary to remove him from Anne's notice. In sending him abroad, I have robbed myself of a good loyal friend, but … I misliked the favour she showed him. Her brother, George, steps forward.

"My tune is best, Your Majesty, don't you agree?"

He picks up a lute and strums a few bars until Norris intercedes.

"No, no, George, the merriment of your tune is quite out of alignment with the sombre mood of the lyric. I think it would be better thus …"

He takes the lute and begins a subtler tune, making cows' eyes at the queen as he sings a few lines of the sonnet. "What do you think, Sire?"

My hand wanders down my wife's back, takes refuge in the curve of her waist, obliging her to step closer to me. The stiff brocade of her gown denies the living flesh beneath, but I know it is there, and I know I must forego the pleasure of enjoying it.

"I like neither tune," I reply. "I shall compose one myself. Here, give me the instrument."

Norris concedes to his king and, within half an hour, I have produced a short tune that is far superior to either of theirs. I feel better now; my mood softens as my cup is refilled and as swiftly emptied.

Christmas is not far away, and Anne busies herself with planning the revels. She has ever had a love for music and dance, and I am gratified that her quicksilver mind is distracted from other, political matters. I, however, am allowed no respite and spend long hours closeted with Cromwell and the rest of the Privy Council.

Before we embarked on this scheme, I'd never appreciated the minutiae of detail required when making changes to almost fifteen hundred years of worship. As the company begins to droop with fatigue, I bring the meeting to an end.

Only Cromwell lingers.

As ever, he is quietly insistent, pressing his opinion, urging me to sign a warrant for the arrest of religious men who refuse to conform. I put down the pen, lean back in my seat and ruffle my hair.

"I am tired, Cromwell. We will continue this tomorrow."

Although he concedes graciously enough, I can tell he is piqued, but it is not his place to demand things of me. It should be the other way around, but it seldom is.

I push the papers away.

"I need to speak to the queen," I say. "I've not seen her since yesterday. She grows impatient if I am absent from her for too long."

Placing both hands on the desk, I push myself to my feet. "I shall see you in the morning, Cromwell."

He bows low and, as I pass him, he begins tidying up his papers.

The doors are opened at my approach, and I pull up short to find one of Anne's women hovering outside the chamber.

"What?" I say, more sharply than I intend when I note her red eyes. "Why have you been weeping? Is the queen ill?"

"No, Your Majesty. The queen is well but ... I fear ... oh, she will be so distressed." Her face crumples into ugly lines. I take her elbow, leading her back into the chamber where she sniffles into a handkerchief.

"Come," I say, irritably. "Come, Mistress, stop your snivelling and give me the news."

"Oh, Your Majesty, it is Purkoy ... he ..."

"Purkoy? What has he done now? Bitten one of the women?"

"No. Oh, Your Majesty, he is *dead*. He must have fallen ... from the window ..."

My breath catches in my throat. Purkoy dead? Anne! Anne will be distraught. My son! She must not be upset.

"The queen; does she know?"

The woman shakes her head.

"We dare not tell her, Your Majesty. That is why I have come to beg you to impart the news yourself. We all lack the courage."

My heart quails a little. Anne is unpredictable. Her grief may be expressed in a gently tragic way or, more likely, she will fly into a rage, and Anne in a rage is something to be avoided. No wonder her women are begging me to do it.

I pat the woman's arm, which I notice is pleasingly plump. "There, there," I say. "Dry your eyes. You may accompany me to the queen so that you are on hand should she need anything I cannot provide. Where is she?"

"Closeted with her seamstress, I believe, Your Majesty."

As we hurry along the corridor, the woman is forced to quicken her pace to keep up with mine. As we go, she keeps up a frantic chatter, explaining how she returned to the queen's chambers to take Purkoy outside for 'some air', as she delicately puts it.

"I couldn't find him, Your Majesty. As you know, he usually runs up barking to anyone who enters, so I knew at once that something was wrong … and then I noticed a cushion on the floor … near the open window. I looked out … and there he was, far below on the gravel. I could tell at once he was …"

The door to a small chamber is opened to admit me and, when I enter, Anne and a few of her women look up from a table piled with bolts of fabric.

"Henry? What is the matter? What are you doing here?"

"Come," I say. "Come with me. We must talk."

She dumps an armful of scarlet onto the table.

"What have I done now?" she demands as I escort her to our private quarters. "Why is your face so grim? Has somebody died? Oh, it isn't Elizabeth, is it?"

"Our daughter is fine."

I send the servants away, press Anne to sit down. I take her hand and pat it, but she snatches it away.

"What is the matter, Henry?"

Her eyes are dark and glinting with fear. I know how quickly her fear can transform into anger. This is not going to be a pretty or comfortable exchange.

"You must stay calm."

"What?" she shrieks, like a guttersnipe. "Tell me!"

"It is Purkoy."

"Purkoy?" Her eyebrows shoot upward and her face floods with relief. "What has he done, jumped up and torn your best hose? Bitten your Fool?"

I ignore her levity. Pat her hand again. Close my eyes.

"He has met with an accident, Anne. He is …"

She leaps up, pushes past me.

"Where is he? Is he hurt badly? Take me to him. Why on earth did you bring me here? I should be with him."

"My love, my love, you can do no good. He has gone."

I grab for her hands again, holding them firm this time.

"Gone?"

For a moment, she is calm, and I think it is going to be all right. I take a deep breath.

"He fell from the window. His death would have been instantaneous. It was just a horrible accident."

She does not blink; her features do not move. For several seconds it is as if she has been turned to stone, but then her mouth opens, her face deforms, her lips squared and ugly, spittle flying.

"An accident?" she screams. "Do you really believe that? Are you really such a gullible fool? It was Catherine, or those who love her and hate me. It was vengeance. I have enemies, Henry, if you'd only admit it, and they must be destroyed. You must not allow them to thrive."

As she spins on her heel and runs from the room, I reach out to catch her arm, but she is too swift and wrenches away, leaving me clasping her velvet, pearl-encrusted sleeve. I should follow and ensure she calms down but … that is what her women are for. I look down, fiddle with a pearl-ringed ruby on her abandoned sleeve, and acknowledge for the first time that I lack the strength, or perhaps the will, to reason with her.

Continuing resistance to the religious changes takes me by surprise, but the strength of protest and their venom against me and my advisors cannot be tolerated. Our attempts at enforcement result in a group of rebellious monks being sentenced to die on the scaffold. I am shaken more than I care to admit by the whole affair, and cannot help but think what Grandmother would have thought. But I hide my discomfort. Treason is treason, whether it comes from a man of God or a dog, and the punishment is the same. But even so, they were *holy* men … I drown my lack of ease in a swathe of merriment and jousts and try not to think of my grandmother's friend, John Fisher, in his cold, lonely cell in the Tower of London.

"Do not hurt him too much, Cromwell," I say when he is taken, "just tease him enough to make him swear the oath. He has ever been a faithful subject; he will do as his king wishes. I am sure of it."

Cromwell bows his head.

"He is stubborn, Your Majesty, but I will see he is persuaded."

I thrust my thoughts from imagining the methods of Cromwell's persuasion. John Fisher is a good man, an old friend, my erstwhile mentor, and I am loath to lose him. *Why can he not just do our bidding?*

I am his king!

And Fisher is not alone in his defection. My old friend, Thomas More, has absented himself from our court. He and I have been at odds about this for a while, but I can no longer ignore it. It was bad enough that he defended Kate during our divorce, and refused to attend Anne's coronation; in fact, sometimes it seems he goes out of his way to offend me.

He is obdurate, stubborn, and extremely unwise in the treasonous path he has chosen. But, after a sleepless night, I decide to make one more attempt to reason with him before he is taken into custody.

It is early morning when I quietly travel upriver to visit him at his Chelsea home. Once the barge bumps against the wharf, I disembark and gaze across his lovely gardens, tilt my face up to his many-windowed palace.

He has risen high beneath my rule, higher than he'd have imagined in my father's day. He is prosperous, his family is vast, and they all have much to lose.

I have barely taken two steps along the path when he appears suddenly from behind a hedge, with a half-grown girl at his side.

"Your Majesty!"

They are taken by surprise, astonished to see me, and both hesitate before sinking to their knees. I pause to allow the difference in our status to sink in, giving them time to reconsider the error of their ways.

Perhaps it would have been kinder to have sent a messenger ahead to warn of my visit. I have caught Thomas in workaday clothes, and his companion, whom I presume to be one of his daughters, has not bothered to properly cover her hair.

"Get up, get up," I say at last, and they rise and approach me.

"This is a welcome surprise, Your Majesty. You will remember my daughter, Margaret?"

She curtseys again and I realise she is not a girl at all, but a full-grown woman, albeit small and plain. She has the grace to blush and look discomforted under my scrutiny.

"May we offer you refreshment, Your Majesty?" she says, opening an arm in the direction of the house.

"Some wine, perhaps, but … have it brought out here, would you? I have some … business with your father."

Her white face pales further but she dips another curtsey and hurries obediently toward the house.

As Thomas guides me along the path between his burgeoning rose beds, I try not to dwell upon happier times. I have been here many times before. Today, although the bushes are stiff with green leaves and fat buds, they are naked of blooms, but I know that soon the garden will be full of fragrance and colour. Our feet leave a dark trail through the dew-soaked grass.

"Thomas, Thomas," I say at last, speaking quietly so as not to disturb the quiet of the morning. "Will you not just swear the oath? For me? Can you not just do it for me, your old friend?"

I peer into his face, but he cannot or will not meet my eye. He does not reply for so long and the silence grows so heavy that I am forced to speak again.

"I thought you my loyal friend and servant ..."

"I am, I am ..."

He looks up earnestly, his forehead furrowed, his eyes haunted. He twists his fingers together. "I am your most loyal servant, but ... I am God's servant first, Your Majesty, and in all conscience I cannot ..."

His eyes fall away again, his shoulders slump as a ball of angry nausea lodges in my chest.

"You know the consequence, Tom? You know what must happen if you refuse to comply? I cannot make allowances for you just because you are my friend."

He nods, looks away from me, across the gardens to the green curve of the river where the pennants of my barge flap feebly in the breeze.

"And you seek a martyr's crown."

He shakes his head but cannot speak, not even in his own defence.

For all the years I have known him, Thomas has championed the Pope, the church, the ways of Rome. All those years ago, it was *his* teaching that prompted me to write in the church's defence, the words that earned me the title Defender of the Faith. A title of which, at the time, I was inordinately proud. Well, the church in Rome has changed and I think differently now. I defend the *faith* with all my heart, but not the Pope and his ravenous flock of carrion crows.

I look down at Thomas' bowed head, his thinning hair streaked with grey, and a deep sorrow envelops me.

I am powerless before his determination.

Thomas cannot abide heresy and they say he has tortured those who embrace the new learning. He sees it as his mission to turn them from sin. Perhaps he will have more empathy for his victims once the thumbscrews are turned on him.

"They will come within the day to take you to the Tower," I say quietly. "This visit is my last attempt to sway you, to save your life. There is nothing more I can do to help you escape it."

Half of me intends it as a warning. I want him to run, to take his sprawling family and flee our shores but, deep down, I know he will never do that. Misguided as he is, he remains a man of honour, and he will be keen to show his colours. The stubborn fool will not miss the opportunity to drive his point home, even if it costs his own life to do it.

Voices float across the garden and we both look toward the house, where Margaret and her mother are hurrying toward us, a servant in their wake bearing a tray. Margaret has changed her gown and hidden her hair beneath a neat gabled hood like her mother's. Reluctantly, I lay a hand on Thomas' shoulder.

"I will not stay. Make your farewells to the family and … thank your women for the offer of refreshments."

My heart is sick within me as I walk briskly toward the waiting barge. My throat constricts, and a tear falls upon my cheek. Never again will I share his company, never again will I greet him as a friend, never again share with him intellectual or spiritual debate. I stumble aboard and keep my face turned from Thomas, who watches me go, his family gathered around him.

I sink upon the waiting cushions.

"Draw the curtains," I say, desperate that no prying eye should witness my grief. As the barge pulls slowly into midstream, I tear off my cap and dash it against the seat, and watch the water of the Thames pass by, as muddy and dark as my breaking heart.

Many men die, but it is John Fisher who is the first. Some say he does it well, but I abhor the manner of his death, and the betrayal of his last words that condemn me as an anti-Christ.

He complains of his treatment by the Tower gaolers and restates his belief that I have no right to the title *Head of the Church in England*. It appals me that a man can show such arrogance, such stubbornness in the face of death, but the matter is out of my hands. Traitors must die; there is nothing I can do to prevent it.

It does not take long for me to discover that the new Pope, Paul III, is no better than the last. He too joins the Catholic faction that hunts me down and tries to tarnish my name. When he realises he is powerless to save Fisher from a traitor's death, in a bid to compound my so-called 'crime,' he creates him 'cardinal.' But a traitor is a traitor and cardinals are no exception.

Anger rages like fire through me, stoking my quiet regret into a loud, righteous fury. I stand fast, hold my own against this duplicitous Pope and refuse to allow the cardinal's hat into the country.

"Once Fisher's head is struck off," I declare, "I will have it sent to Rome where the bishop and his crows can anoint it at their leisure!"

My hands tremble, my voice not as steady as it should be, and Cromwell, seeing it, surreptitiously pushes a cup toward me. I drain it, and wipe a trickle of wine from my beard.

"Damn the Pope," I growl. "And damn Fisher too. Damn them all to hell."

But, after the deed is done and word is sent that they are dead, I sit alone in the darkness and wonder at the speed with which events are taking place.

What happened to the church I loved, the absolute obedience I once gave the Pope? Has the world altered so much, or have I?

Noting my gloom, the queen and her friends prepare for a pageant to distract me, and while they do so, I start to look inward, examining the type of monarch I am becoming.

It was never my intention to be a cruel ruler. I always planned to be a benign and merry king; a man beloved of his people, yet … if they refuse to be ruled by me, refuse to love me, there is nought I can do but strike back. They must be made to realise who is king and who subject.

I am surrounded by gloom these days. How is it that I am here in darkness while my queen dances with other men in the sunshine?

It is almost June, the merry month of May is all but over, and tomorrow the sun will shine. I've had enough of this incessant conflict; these dour days must be gone, and I must ensure a brighter path lies ahead.

I sit up straighter, clap my hands, and a page comes running.

"Send for the master of revels and give the order for a picnic tomorrow. We shall hunt in the morning and feast after noon. Order up musicians and dancers; prepare the fools, and the minstrels. Let us pour some happiness into this dreary summer. It is about time England became merry again."

In the morning, I instruct them to lay out my brightest clothes. I put on my favourite hat and order the grooms to saddle up my fastest mare. Anne, still yawning from her night of revels, is at my side and, together with our combined households, we set off across the countryside.

There is nothing lovelier than England in the early summer. The bluebells are over now but in their place are the frothy blooms of cow parsley, the red splash of a nodding poppy as we thunder by. We pound across the heath and into the forest, where the fragrant scents of the moor give way to the earthier tang of loam and bracken.

The game is shy today, but it does not really matter. I am glad to be out of the palace, to feel the fresh air in my lungs. I breathe deeply, look about for my companions who, as always, can barely keep up with me. They are lagging far behind.

I miss Brandon. He would keep pace with me, but he is not yet returned from France. I must order his return home. As always, when I think of Charles, my thoughts turn to my dead sister, and I feel a pang of sadness. So many have died, yet I miss Mary more than any other. She was taken too young;

she was far too important to leave me, and she leaves a void that cannot be filled.

I am affronted that God saw fit to take her.

"I swear, I've not seen a single rabbit let alone deer," Anne says as she trots up, mounted on the fattest, slowest horse in the stable.

Her face is red from the sun. She comes to a halt beside me and smiles breathlessly as she attempts to remove a stray strand of hair that has become tangled across her face. I lean forward to assist her.

"Thank you, Henry," she says. "Shall we dismount? I feel a little … odd."

"Unwell?"

Immediately alert, I slide from the saddle and assist her to the ground. "I said you should not come. You are too strong-headed, madam."

"It is just the heat, Henry, do not fuss so …"

She pauses mid-sentence and puts a hand to her stomach.

"What is it? Is it the child?"

Her face is now white, the bones of her face rigid, the veins on her temple blue, her teeth clenching her lower lip. She bends forward, clutches my sleeve.

"Anne!"

She looks up, speaks through clenched teeth.

"I must return to the palace. Now!"

So, another son is lost. As so many times before, I must put away my dreams and longings and present a brave face to the world. At least Anne did not die, I tell myself; I must be grateful for that. Everyone is telling me that she is strong and will quickly rally.

We can try again soon.

I try not to blame her for attending the hunt against my advice, against my express wishes. I wish I could unleash my simmering anger, but it will do little good. There is no point in alienating Anne, tainting our relationship with blame and recrimination. The child has gone. At least we still have time.

But it takes all my willpower not to slump into despondency. To cheer myself and to prove to the world that I am carefree, I demand ever more summer entertainments; tournaments and tennis, minstrels in the garden, dancing in the meadow, and slowly the forced jollity begins to work and, to those who matter, my high spirits seem genuine.

Anne emerges from her chambers, somewhat paler and somewhat more subdued, so I spoil her with dainties, ply her with gifts. Her old smile is slow to return but she is kinder now, softer somehow, and instead of demanding great feats from me in our bed, she clings like a child in search of succour. She craves comfort where once she demanded excitement.

I miss her old vibrancy.

"It will return, Your Majesty," Cromwell says when I finally confide my troubles to him. "It was much the same with my wife …"

I glance up quickly. He rarely mentions his family, the wife and small girls who perished of the sweat some years ago. Although his suffering must have been great, nobody would guess it for he never lets it show. His loss has not scarred him. He is pragmatic. Life, as they say, goes on.

It is probably better not to remark on it.

"I've done all I can to cheer the queen. She thinks she has failed me … she has, I suppose, but we must carry on. She is back in my bed but … It is our duty to conceive again as soon as we can."

Somehow, duty removes the pleasure.

"Perhaps a change of scene, Sire. A short progress to the country?"

"It might do the trick, yes. Even a visit to Hatfield; some time spent with our daughter might cheer her."

When our morning's work is done and Cromwell departs, I go in search of Anne but find her apartments empty. I stand in the centre of the floor and survey the deserted rooms. Usually, even in her absence, her apartments are busy; her servants taking the opportunity to restore order, plumping cushions, stoking the fires, so the rooms are comfortable on her return, but today there is no one.

I wait, relishing the rare moment alone and acknowledge how eerily quiet it is without the constant clamour with which the queen surrounds herself.

I am aware of distant clashing of pans from the kitchens, a servant calling, someone singing, discordant and merry in the garden. There is a dog barking just outside the window, someone hollering at it to shut up, and then another small sound, a furtive sound that is much closer, in this very room. The hair on the back of my neck prickles as goosebumps march across my skin. I turn my head sharply from side to side, my eyes swivelling to determine where the sound is coming from. The sound of … breathing.

I am not alone after all.

Warily, with fear scuttling like a spider up my back, I turn my head. There is no one here, nothing I can see, nothing of this world. But I know I am watched. I can feel it.

I hold my breath, stand still like a statue, and the room is so silent that when something drops and rolls across the floor toward me, I squeak with fear.

Assassin! The word hisses in my brain, my mouth drying, any call for help strangled in my throat. I leap back, heart racing like a hare's as something small and metallic settles at my feet. But, after regarding it for a moment, I stoop to pick it up and squint at the thimble that perches like a fool's cap on the tip of my finger.

Assassin? I trace the path from whence it came, and the trail ends at the bottom of a curtain from which a pair of black-toed shoes are peeping.

Assassins do not carry thimbles. In two paces, I cross the room and tear back the curtain. A woman gasps.

A small plain woman with huge stricken eyes. She falls to her knees, like a felled sapling in a sapphire blue pool. Quickly, she lowers her head, spreads out her arms.

"I beg pardon, Your Majesty, I was afraid … I didn't know … what I should do."

I hold out the thimble.

"I think you dropped this."

She rises slowly and shakily to her feet and fixes her eye on her lost thimble.

"Yes. I dropped it."

She doesn't look me in the eye and her wish to escape my presence is plain, but she is pleasing, and I am bored. I decide to tease her a little before I grant her release.

"I mistook you for an assassin, Mistress; you are fortunate I drew back the curtain before I ran you through with my sword."

She risks glancing up at my face, her eyes even bigger than before. She swallows and blinks, knotting and unknotting her fingers as she fumbles for the right words.

"I am very sorry I startled you, Your Majesty."

"Apology accepted. You almost frightened the life out of me. Look, feel how fast my heart races."

I take her hand and hold it against my chest. She nods agreement although the chances of her detecting my heartbeat through my padded doublet are slim indeed. "And your name is?"

"Jane. Jane Seymour."

"Of Wulf Hall; you are Edward's sister?"

She nods. "Yes, that's right, Your Majesty."

"And your business here?"

She glances again at my finger where her thimble still perches, and realising I have yet to return it, I place it ceremonially on hers. She wrinkles her nose when she smiles.

"The queen sent me to fetch her thimble. The weather is so fine the ladies have taken their sewing into the garden."

"A good idea. I might join you, but first ..."

"Yes, Your Majesty?"

"I would beg a favour of you."

She blushes as she warily nods.

"Give me the thimble to deliver to my wife while you run to my chambers and fetch my spaniels. They could do with a run. You're not afraid of dogs, are you?"

"Yes, Your Majesty. No, Your Majesty."

She passes back the thimble and sinks to her knees again.

"Go, go, go …" I smile benignly, flick my fingers, and watch her run away.

A funny, quaint little woman, past her first flush but she has a certain appeal; an innocent woman, free from ire.

Pocketing the thimble, I head for the gardens, the sun blinding me as I emerge from the darkness of the palace. As I grow near, servants pause in their tasks, doing their best to become invisible as they bow low over their burdens until I have passed.

As Jane had directed, I discover the queen in her favourite corner of the rose garden, her women surrounding her like diamonds around a ruby in a royal ring. A perfect setting.

Anne looks up at my approach, holds a finger to her lips, instructing me not to interrupt the plaintive song her minstrel is singing. I push my annoyance aside and assume interest in the melody.

Mark Smeaton, dark and disgustingly youthful, plucks his lute, his rich baritone silencing the summer birds. I notice that all the women, my wife included, have let their sewing fall to their laps and have turned as one to listen to him. They are all enthralled. Quietly, I take my seat beside Anne and pass her the thimble.

"Is there anything else my queen desires?" I ask, in playful tones. She allows the dimple in her right cheek to show, a glimpse of her old humour emerging.

"You make a fine lady's maid, Sire. What have you done with Jane, sent her to the Tower?"

I snort.

"I think I might enjoy being your tiring-woman. The thought of making you ready for the night has a certain appeal."

She flaps a hand at me.

"If I know you, my lord, you'd dispense with brushing my hair or putting scent behind my ears just to skip to the moment of my unrobing."

"Possibly. I see no need for preliminaries."

Our eyes meet, mine lusty with longing, hers hesitant … shy, perhaps? Or a little reluctant? She wets her lips, a smile trembling her cheek before she drops her gaze again and leans closer to speak directly into my ear.

"If you wish, I could send all my attendants away early tonight, if you'd care to try out the position of tiring-woman."

My answering smile is wide as delight unfurls in my belly.

"Consider the bargain sealed, Mistress. I will attend you at eight."

"Supper will barely be over by then."

"I am but an apprentice maid and will need a great deal of tutoring in the task."

I peer surreptitiously down the top of her bodice to the swell of her bosom, slyly inhaling her scent. She flaps a hand at me.

"Do not sniff me, Sir, I am not a nosegay. But yes, come to me at eight and I will teach you the lesson gladly, my lord."

She laughs as she turns back to the singing. I slip my hand into hers and feign delight in Smeaton's performance too.

Anne slips from her loose over-gown, nonchalantly hands it to me and points to a clothes press.

"First you must choose a nightgown."

I open the door, inhaling the scents of lavender and rosemary, a hint of camphor. I pull out a silken garment, embroidered at neck and cuff with small red flowers, and lay it carefully on the bed as I have seen my own servants do. Then, I turn, clasp my hands, and smile meekly and insipidly, like a maid.

She laughs loudly in a rather undignified manner for a queen, before turning away to study her face in the looking glass.

"Now you must unlace my kirtle."

I move closer, peer at the web of tight lacing and wonder how I should proceed. I cannot locate the end of the thread so, fetching the candle from her nightstand, I bring it closer.

"Your hair is in the way."

"Your Majesty."

"Eh?"

"You must address me as 'Your Majesty, for I am your queen and you are but a lowly servant.'"

Obligingly, she raises her arms, scoops her hair up and exposes her long neck, strands of dark hair, a small mole. I long to kiss it but this game is rich and I want to prolong it, for the chase is always better than the kill.

Following the line of her spine, I eventually spy the end of a lace aglet peeking from the top of her kirtle. Taking it between finger and thumb, I pull gently and begin to draw it through the holes, quicker and quicker, one by one, inch by inch, until her bodice is loosened. When I reach the small of her back, where her torso curves and spreads into her buttocks, my heart begins to beat more strongly. I pause and swallow.

Take a deep breath and await further instruction.

"Now, you must slide it from my shoulders. Do not drop the garment on the floor, you must hold it while I step from it and then place it on the chair."

I do as I am bid, and when she has moved aside, I lay the kirtle with the gown over the back of a chair. She turns to face me and flips her hair from her shoulders. Clad only in her shift, her body is clearly discernible through the fine, diaphanous linen. I feel a stirring. I could take her now. She could not deny me; I am her king and her husband.

But, as if she reads my thoughts, she holds a finger aloft.

"Do not forget I am your queen, and you are my servant, Sir."

I nod, pushing my desire into the pit of my being while she sits down and lifts the hem of her shift to reveal her hose, and the soft skin above. With dry mouth, I kneel at her feet, my fingers suddenly thick and clumsy as I fumble to untie her garters. The womanly scent of her body rises, the warmth of her skin heating me further. Inflaming my desire. I long to kiss the warm, soft flesh of her thigh, but I tell myself 'No.' I am her maid, and she is my queen. I must not think ahead, I must force myself to concentrate on the matter in hand.

Trying not to snag the fine silk, I unroll the hose, draw it from her foot, almost drooling when, provocatively, she wiggles her pink toes. While blood pumps furiously in my ears, I clamber to my feet and endeavour to stand obediently and wait for further instruction.

She lifts her arms, enabling me to pull the shift over her head and, as I do so, her hair, so full of vitality, unleashes and winds itself in my fingers, clings to my clothes. We are standing very close now. Face to face. I can feel her breath on my cheek and, when I raise my eyes to hers, I find they are huge and very dark, and full of longing.

"Your Majesty, am I a male servant, or a female?"

Her eyes open wide as the tip of her tongue emerges. She moistens her lips and I know she wants this as much as I. She ignores my question.

"Now, you must sponge me," she says, her face full of devilment, "… all over."

She indicates a bowl of scented water on her nightstand, and a large sponge beside it. I pick it up, squeeze moisture from it, water running up my sleeve as I turn to look at her. She is naked, perched regally on her seat, her hair loose about her shoulders like a black silk shroud, her nipples dark and stunningly erect. Her eyes that a short time ago were full of mockery now smoulder with lust. My heart pounds so quickly the roaring in my ears is deafening, and I am so stiff in the nethers that I can bear no more.

I take a step closer, throw down the sponge.

"Sponge be damned," I say. "There'll be time for washing after I am done with you."

Within weeks, Anne is back to her old self. We argue and make love in turn; she infuriates yet obsesses me at the same time. I hate her in the morning and long to tup her by the afternoon. It is as if some devil has me in a snare, as if she is master and I the slave. Everything changes, however, when in early October she confides that she may be pregnant once more.

At once, the old dreams and plans return and, despite urging myself to show caution for all might yet be lost, my spirits rise. Even the continuing nonsense from Mary and Kate cannot dull my good mood.

For a few months, despite the early sickness, Anne is serene; she is a queen, shortly to birth a prince, but as the demands of her great belly begin to tell, the queen's temper begins to fray.

She snaps and snarls at everyone like a whelping bitch, and there are daily arguments and disagreements. I find myself making excuses, avoiding her company. I cannot share her bed for fear of injuring the child, and since I have no wish to join her companions in her apartments, I seek out my own friends and take note of those who have strayed from my company into Anne's.

The wait for my son is long, and I am not a patient man. Without a woman in my bed, I grow bored and lonely and, although I try to resist, the need for female company is strong.

Before too many months have passed, I have made sure to encounter Margery, who offered me her comfort before. She is glad to take up where we left off and I am glad to be spared the necessity of persuading her. She is neither the prettiest nor the wittiest woman at my court, but she is buxom and willing. We exchange very little in the way of conversation but, after dark, with the candles extinguished, she fills a need, and I send her off satisfied. Her purse is a little fatter when I am done.

If Anne is aware of it, she knows better than to complain. Her duty is to provide me with an heir and then I will gladly take her back into my bed, until such time as we conceive another. It is not her body I miss so much as her conversation, for her mind is, or used to be, as lithe and as wicked as her naughty tongue. Margery may fill Anne's absence, but she is slow, comfortable and does not stimulate my mind. For that, I must wait until I can be with Anne again.

I miss the games we played. I miss the jokes we shared in the days before she grew snappish. These days, when I approach her apartments in search of intellectual debate, I am met with hostility, and I am certain she takes the opposite point of view in any discussion just to provoke me.

The new English Bible is a case in point. She applauds it, believing it is a good thing that man can read the word of God without the intercession of a priest. I disagree. There are few educated men who can perfectly interpret the truths the Bible holds. Even if a ploughman did possess the ability to read the words, he'd lack the wit to understand them. It is one thing to read the words of a message, yet quite another to comprehend it.

"But, Henry," she retorts infuriatingly, "who is to say a king has the right interpretation? There are many differing explanations that can be drawn from a single passage of the Bible. Perhaps, for all his lack, the ploughman is right, and the king mistaken. Had you thought of that?"

I leap to my feet.

"Mistaken? A king is never mistaken, Madam. He may be misled, he may be misinterpreted, he may be misunderstood, but he is never *wrong*, for he is king, and God's messenger on Earth. It is God who plants the thoughts in my head; how can I be wrong?"

She laughs, dismissively, mockingly, and I am filled with sudden rage. I narrow my eyes; thrust my face menacingly toward hers.

"But a *queen* can be wrong, Madam, as you should bear in mind, and learn from experience. A *queen* can be very wrong!"

I storm from the chamber, ignoring her placating tones calling me back. As I barge through the doors, I tell myself I am done with her company. She has no right to mock me or to question the validity of my opinions.

Her job is to do as she is told.

Swiftly, I turn a corner and cannon into a small figure who staggers backward, fights to regain balance before sprawling onto the floor. I am instantly contrite.

"Oh, Madam, I beg pardon. Here, take my hand. Let me help you."

Small, slim fingers slide into my palm, and I haul her to her feet. She brushes her skirts, sinks into a curtsey, and then another, her head bobbing up and down like a cork in a river.

"It was my fault, Your Majesty. I do beg pardon."

"Oh, it's Jane, isn't it? We met before, behind the curtain …" I peer through the gloom of the torches, recognising the calm eyes, the soothing expression.

"Yes, Your Majesty." She bobs again, reluctantly meeting my eye. I give her my best smile.

"We do seem to meet in odd circumstances. I hope you are unharmed. Walk with me into the light so we may be sure there are no bruises."

I take her elbow and propel her toward a window, turn her to face me. She is a funny little thing, so meek, so pleasant, and so uncritical.

"Now, where does it hurt?"

She lifts her right arm. "I think I banged my elbow but other than that, I am unscathed, Your Majesty."

"Show me."

I take her arm and unlace her sleeve, draw it off that I may roll up the sleeve of her shift. The skin on her arm is pale, untouched by the sun, in all probability untouched by man.

I smooth my fingers along the light down of hair and come to rest on a mole at the elbow. "Where does it hurt?" I turn the arm, and see a graze at the joint, the beginnings of a bruise. "Hmm, come with me. I have just the thing for that."

She follows me silently to my apartment; my servants melt away when they notice my companion is female. I should bid them stay but I don't.

Jane follows me to my still-room, the place where I dry my herbs, prepare and store my medicines and salves. She hovers in the middle of the carpet, like a deer that longs to run but knows the hound is fleeter.

I rummage among the jars on my shelf and pick one up in triumph.

"Here it is, this will soothe and help heal." I indicate that she should remove her sleeve again and dab a little ointment on the sore place. "I've always been fascinated with herbs and medicine. My grandmother taught me the basics when I was a boy, and I have maintained the interest. Is it beginning to work?"

I haven't released her arm for I am too aware of the softness of her skin, and the way her trembling is fanning the flame of my interest.

"I think it is working."

She glances up with a fearful smile. "It is fortunate my sleeves are so thick, or the skin may have been broken."

"We must drink together," I say, releasing her arm and pouring us each a cup of wine. She takes the cup, sips tentatively and nods her appreciation.

"That's the best wine you've tasted, I warrant."

"It is, Your Majesty."

"Henry." I speak quietly but she steps back, puts down the cup and shakes her head.

"Oh, I could never address you so, Your Majesty. The queen would …"

"The queen be damned."

She gasps, mouth slightly open, her breath rapid.

"Jane, I would just like to talk. You have nothing to fear, your virtue is safe with me. Sit, there. Speak with me."

She does as I bid. No argument, no clever riposte, no challenge. I give her back the cup.

"What would you like to talk about?" She sips delicately.

"What is your opinion on the new learning? This new English Bible?"

Silence follows, the fire crackles as I wait for her to think of the correct answer. She looks down and I follow her gaze to her hands that are tightly wrapped around her cup.

"Do you want an honest answer, Your Majesty or
...?"

I lean forward, my forearms on my knees.

"I do want you to be honest, Jane. You must promise
to always be honest with me."

"Well ..." Her tongue comes out again to wet her lips.
"I think it a sin, Your Majesty. I think the devil is behind this
new learning."

"And the reforms?"

"I think they are a mistake, Your Majesty, if you will
forgive me. I think you have been swayed by – by evil men."

"The devil you do!"

I sit up, her terrified eyes meeting mine. Neither of us
blinks and I am surprised to find myself neither angry nor
offended.

"Between you and me, I often wonder if that is so. But
how does one know? How can I be certain? There is
corruption in the church, I know that for a fact, so what
should I do? Allow it to continue? Allow the people to be
fooled, to be cheated?"

A frown mars her pleasant face. Briefly, I consider
asking her to remove her hood that I may discover the shade
and texture of her hair, but I refrain. There will be time for
that. She would only take flight again and I am just beginning
to tame her.

"Perhaps, Your Majesty could engage the churchmen
in discussion. There must be a way to reach some agreement. I
am sure once shown the error of their ways they would happily
change. It is easy for us to fall into sin without realising we are
doing so. They love and honour you as their king; they would
want to please you."

"So, you are a politician, Madam. What of the
corruption of Rome? They will not heed me. Should the wealth
of our realm continue to pass through the conduit of the holy
church into the coffers of the Pope?"

"I- I," she whimpers, out of her depth, and springs to
her feet, distressed by my sudden bitterness. "I do not know,
Your Majesty. I am sorry, I am not a scholar."

I take hold of her arm.

"It is I who should apologise. You are but a simple maid, how should you know the answers to questions that perplex the greatest minds in Europe? I brought you here to soothe me and all I have done is ruffle you. Do you like music? Would you like me to play?

1536

The year 1536 blows in hard and cold. For too long we are incarcerated in the palace. As soon as it is fine enough to ride out, I order up the hunt. The good clean air in my lungs clears my head, chases away the megrim, and I am reinvigorated, like a new man.

"Hopefully, January will be softer from now on," I remark to Brandon while we pause our ride to allow our horses to rest. "I am glad you have returned to court. There is nothing worse for the mind than idleness."

"I agree. The tournament will begin in a few weeks; we must put in some extra practise in the tiltyard."

"We must." I pull off my cap and enjoy the breeze in my hair. "Still fancy your chances of besting me, do you?"

He laughs, turns to look at me. I notice lines about his eyes, and there are strands of grey in his beard.

"Oh, I've long given up any hope of that, Sire."

We both recognise the lie and as we make our slow way home, our conversation turns to other things.

Since I took Anne to wife, Brandon has spent less time at court. I suspect he has not forgiven me for spurning Kate, and I know Mary deplored my break with her, and died with bitterness toward me in her heart.

Anne pretends she doesn't mind the disdain; ostentatiously, she spurns Brandon's company and sneers if I speak of him. But I miss him nonetheless and wish my wife and best friend could be reconciled. For my sake if not their own.

"We will joust on Tuesday," I say. "I have a meeting with the Spanish ambassador in the morning, but he is only stirring more trouble on behalf of my errant daughter, Mary. I will ensure the meeting is no longer than it need be."

"I shall look forward to it, Sire, and remember to close your visor this time."

I roar with laughter at his reference to a former joust when the tip of his lance clipped my open visor and filled my helmet with splintered wood. It was a close-run thing, yet the day ended well.

His handsome face alive with humour, Brandon gathers his reins, sits forward in the saddle, ready to ride. "I'll race you back to the stables."

Throwing my hat into the wind, I take the challenge; whip my horse's rump with the end of the reins. Five minutes later as we career into the yard, he is a neck behind. I haul my mount to a halt and turn to Brandon laughing.

"There, I beat you, hands down!"

"By a nose, Your Majesty! Only by a nose."

I look about for a servant, slide from the saddle and throw the reins to a groom. As I turn to wait for Brandon to catch up, a messenger wearing Cromwell's livery dashes to my side.

"Your Majesty," he grovels, head down. "My master wishes to see you urgently."

My heart sinks. Am I allowed no leisure?

"Why, what is it?"

He hesitates, his dry lips quivering. A suspicious-looking sore on the side of his mouth is weeping, in need of salve.

"Tell me now, boy. What is the matter?"

"It is the queen, Your Majesty. She is dead."

The world tips. I grab for Brandon's sleeve, my voice stolen along with my breath. Brandon holds me tightly, his strong arms bracing me, preventing my collapse.

"What do you mean, dead?" he snarls. "She was right as rain this morning."

The boy's face blanches. He gapes at us with horror.

"A thousand pardons, Your Majesty. I - I meant. Not the *queen* – I meant the Dowager Princess of Wales. I am sorry to have – have …"

My head ceases pounding, my breathing steadies as my mind slowly rights itself, and the sudden grief in my heart is replaced with another gentler sorrow.

"Kate is dead?"

My voice is hoarse.

"Ah." Brandon removes his hat, looks at the ground. "May she rest in peace."

I look at him, his face blurs.

"Amen," I whisper. "Amen. I – I had no idea she was sick … well, not sick unto death."

"Did Chapuys not tell you so?"

I do not miss the unspoken accusation in his tone, but I am too stunned to react to it. Chapuys did indeed inform me that Kate was ailing again, but she was always complaining, I thought it was just another grievance. She has harped on about cold damp castles and neglect ever since I left the sham that was our marriage.

For all her grievances, the expense of keeping her and her huge household has been a burden on me. It will be easier now she has gone, and perhaps now the people will be more accepting of Anne.

But I can't help remembering and grieving for the Kate I first knew; the fair princess who stole my heart when she arrived in England to marry my brother.

The first time I saw her I would never have dreamed what the future held for us. I certainly never imagined that perfect, happy princess would ever become such a repugnant weight around my neck.

As we turn toward the hall steps, I realise my hands are shaking and the sun is no longer quite so bright, the air chilling rather than bracing. I must tell Anne.

The thought of informing her is unpleasant, almost disrespectful to Kate but … I am being ridiculous. Of course, she must be told.

I instruct Cromwell to ensure that there is no undue mourning at court. We must all remember that the woman who has died was never our true queen, she was not even my wife, she was simply my brother's wife, a dowager princess of a dead prince and an obscure principality.

"Henry! Did you enjoy your ride? I would so much have liked to join you."

Anne rises, leaving her women by the window while she comes forward to receive my kiss, granting Brandon a dismissive nod. He makes the obligatory bow and steps diplomatically back into shadow. I wet my lips and glance about the room to see who is within hearing distance before speaking quietly.

"We have received some news, Anne."

"News? What news?" She cocks her head, her face infused with curiosity, her voice too loud.

"We've had word from Kimbolton."

Her interest palls, she rolls her eyes and shrugs.

"Oh, Catherine! What complaint does she have now?"

Her flippancy ignites my anger.

"No complaint at all. She is dead."

She cannot conceal the momentary look of glee that splashes across her face before she remembers her place, and schools her emotion.

"Oh. Well, it isn't as if we didn't know she was ailing. Perhaps your bastard, Mary, will obey your wishes from now on."

Mary. I had not thought of her. She will be …

"I have some new gowns, Henry. What do you think of this yellow, does it suit me? Or does it make my skin look green?"

I watch, a little stunned by her lack of respect as she twists and turns with her new silk gown held beneath her chin. It is as if I am seeing her for the first time. Kate, for all her sins, was once Anne's mistress. She must have known her well and, in the beginning, Kate would have been kind, and tried to make Anne welcome at our court.

"It becomes you well," I mutter and, as I turn away, I notice Jane, sitting with the other women by the window. Her pale face is stricken, and something moist is glistening on her cheek. She, at least, has the decency to regret the passing of a good woman. I allow her a slight nod before turning back to Anne.

"I must speak with Cromwell. There is much to be arranged. I will return later."

Anne barely registers my departure. Brandon follows me along the corridor but neither of us speaks. I look neither left nor right. My heart is heavy. On one hand, I am relieved that the constant harping and accusations are over. Now Kate has gone there can be no question of Elizabeth's legitimacy. But on the other hand, I am pained at the passing of my erstwhile wife ... although she was, in fact, no wife at all; she was my friend.

Cromwell has the tact to be sombre at the news. He puts his head on one side.

"Death of those we once loved is always difficult," he says, and I find myself touched by the empathy behind his bland words.

"She was not always a difficult woman. Circumstances made her so. Once she was a merry qu- woman."

He clears his throat, takes something from inside his doublet.

"Your Majesty, there is a letter, dictated by the dowager princess during her last hours."

"For me?"

I take it warily between two fingers; certain it will contain further recrimination. Kate would have relished an opportunity to lecture me from beyond the grave. I break the seal and move closer to the window.

My most dear lord, King and husband,

The hour of my death now drawing on, the tender love I owe thou forces me, my case being such, to commend myself to thou, and to put thou in remembrance with a few words of the health and safeguard of thine soul which thou ought to prefer before all worldly matters, and before the care and pampering of thy body, for the which thou have cast me into many calamities and thineselv into many troubles. For my part, I pardon thou everything, and I desire to devoutly pray God that He will pardon thou also. For the rest, I commend unto thou our daughter Mary, beseeching thou to be a good father unto her, as I have heretofore desired. I entreat thou also, on behalf of my maids, to give them marriage portions, which is not much, they being but three. For all mine other servants I solicit the wages due them, and a year more, lest they be unprovided for. Lastly, I make this vow, that mine eyes desire thou above all things.

Katharine the Queen.

I let the letter fall and make a sound that is half laugh and half sob. Blinking rapidly, I look up at Cromwell and, when I speak, to my chagrin my voice rasps with emotion.

"The damned woman has signed herself *Katharine the Queen.*"

But I feel no rancour toward her now. I find, despite everything, that I am touched; bereaved, even. Sadness settles across my shoulders like a mantle, weighing me down with regret. So much bitterness between us. Yet, all those years of argument and discord need never have happened if only she hadn't been so stubborn; or had she only been fertile.

24th January 1536

After weeks of rain, the morning of the joust dawns fine and I am up with the lark, harrying my gentlemen to help me dress. I break my fast, drum my fingers through morning prayers and then I am off, running down the steps, calling for my horse. Brandon and my other gentlemen are at my heels, some of them rubbing their heads and squinting at the sudden intrusion of the sun. I was a wise man and took early to my bed, but others were less prudent and sought darker ways to pass the night.

"What's the matter with you, Bryan, are you still in your cups?"

"No, Sire, but ... it is devilish early, I swear my brain doesn't yet realise my body is up and about. It's still tucked up in bed ..."

I do not miss the wistful look in his eye and wonder which wanton he left behind to keep his sheets warm. A groom comes forward to assist me to mount, and I gather up the reins and laugh at Bryan's feeble attempts to climb into the saddle.

"Call yourself a man? It is lucky you no longer compete, for what chance would you stand at the tilt today if you can barely get your foot in the stirrup?"

The company laughs, Bryan joins in sheepishly, adjusts the patch that covers his damaged eye and pushes back his cap, the feathered brim fluttering in the breeze.

"I will wake up long before we reach the field, Sire, never fear. I am just thankful I only have the one eye to force open."

The resulting laugh is hearty, yet it is really no laughing matter. The long-ago accident at the tilt that cost him his eye could have taken his life. It wouldn't have been the first time a man died at the sport. We are all aware of the danger, but we are men, knights of the field, heroes of the age.

Despite the early hour, the tournament field is already full of people. The crowd mostly consists of men and young boys, eager for the competition. There are a few women who have made the effort to rise early to watch the proceedings, but the royal stand is empty, for the queen will not be attending. I have forbidden her anything that may in any way harm our unborn son. I don't care how much she complains or sulks. She scowled when I took my leave of her.

"There are months yet before the child is born," she declares. "You can't keep me a prisoner!"

"Yes, I can," I call over my shoulder. "I am your husband and your king. I can lock you in the Tower for the rest of your confinement if it pleases me."

I don't care how many months of forced idleness she must endure; this time, *this time*, nothing must prevent the birth of a living boy.

As ever, pregnancy is frustrating for the queen and her mood is grim. Mistress Seymour has reluctantly confessed to me that she receives the brunt of Anne's bad temper. Jane and I have become good friends but as yet she has resisted my efforts to make her my mistress. She is hesitant but I suspect she is merely playing coy, just for show. She wants to appear virtuous lest I and the court mistake her for a whore – it is the same with all women. I know she likes me, and I am determined to overcome it.

As we enter the tiltyard the trumpets sound, and I soak in the applause before dismounting. I wave to the crowd, leap from the saddle and, while the groom leads my horse to the equine armouring tent, I throw back the door of the pavilion and duck inside.

A fire is burning in the brazier, and several boys are seated around it, tightening rivets, checking straps and buckles, and burnishing my armour.

"Make it shine, my good fellows, so I might blind my opponent before he even has time to level his lance."

They pull their forelocks, bend their heads over their work, polishing fervently. I pour my own drink, empty the cup in one draught, and smack my lips.

"Ah, Brandon," I say when he ducks into the tent, picks up a cup and drains it. "It is a fine day for it. We have been too long cooped up inside. I feel in the best form, are you sure you don't wish to withdraw your challenge?"

He puts down his own cup.

"And lose your respect, Sire? Never. But Norris looks the worse for wear and may wish to wriggle out of it."

We both turn to regard Norris who, still bedraggled from lack of sleep and an overindulgence of wine, straightens up and puffs out his chest.

"There is nothing wrong with me. I am fit as a flea."

"Me too," says Bryan, his bloodshot eyes belying his words. "I am a Howard, Sire, we never avoid a challenge."

"That is what I like to hear, even if it is bravado."

He seldom fails to remind me he is close blood cousin to the queen. Some say his position at court is due to her office, yet they are wrong. I like Bryan for all his reprobate ways.

It is time to make ready for the tourney and as I am stripped of my clothes and helped into my gambeson, Brereton, and Francis Weston arrive in the company of the queen's brother, George.

"Apologies for our late arrival, Sire," George bows. "We had trouble rousing ourselves."

"So, you were in the company of Bryan last night, I assume."

He has the grace to hang his head, smile ruefully.

"I swear, Sire, I was led on. I would far rather have been abed."

The boy, having secured my breastplate, reaches for the plackart, and I stand pliant beneath his ministrations. Armouring is always a lengthy business, and I grow impatient while the many buckles are tightened and checked. The other men are similarly made ready.

"Come, come," I say. "Hurry up and fetch my helmet, the day will be done before we reach the tilt."

With much merriment, we exit the tent and emerge into the blue day. A woman, whose face I know but whose name I misremember, comes running forward and offers me her favour.

"In the queen's absence, Your Majesty," she says, and I take it from her, inhale the sweet fragrance before tucking it beneath my breastplate.

My horse is waiting, scraping his hooves and kicking up dust. He is brightly caparisoned in Tudor colours, and when he sees me coming, he sidesteps and rolls his eyes at the flapping pennants and the great noise. I place my hand on his neck and my forehead against his nose, and he seems to calm at the sound of my voice.

"There, that's better."

I am helped to mount, my armour hindering my usual dexterity. Easing into the saddle, I take up the reins, feeling the latent power of the animal beneath me. He is flighty this morning. The weight of my armoured body warms his blood, and he is as prepared as I for the challenge. My horse and I are one, ready to stand against our opponents.

The other four men ride first, the best of each competing one against the other, and then against me, their king. I wait impatiently, reining down hard upon my mount's eagerness to take the field.

Heralds blast their trumpets; the pennants snap in the brisk wind. Brandon takes up his lance, his horse half-rearing, but he brings it down, regains control and levels his lance. Silence, just for a moment, then the crowd roars as the two steeds pound toward each other, the ground shaking, dust flying. A great crash and a cry from the crowd as the lances splinter, one man falls, the other rides away. When the dust clears, the crowd screams with delight.

Their delight, of course, is nothing to what I receive when it is my turn to take the field. The enforced wait has wound my horse's nerves until he is as tight as a trebuchet, and I know he will be hard to hold. We trot forward, his breath rising like a dragon's as he fights against my restraint, burgeoning for action. The trumpets blast again, the crowd's cheers increase. They toss their caps in the air – anticipating my win before I have made it.

I take up the lance, level it, my eye on my opponent at the opposite end of the tilt. The horse snorts, his eager flanks twitching. He paws the ground and tries to rear, but with a curse I hold him fast. The flag drops and instantly I spur him to action. Steadily, remorselessly, we gallop solidly down the field. Through the thin strip of my visor I see a blur of colours, my ears fill with the muffled sounds of the crowd, my horse's hooves beat in time with the rhythm of my heart.

My opponent is reduced to a splash of colour as the tip of his lance grows closer; foam from my horse's mouth flies up onto my visor, obscuring my view, and something canons hard into my shoulder. The breath leaves my lungs as a nightmare ensues: sounds of splintering; screaming. My horse's legs are suddenly weak beneath me; his head comes up and back as my head falls forward. He strikes my helmet, my nose ... he falters, stumbles, and I lose my balance, my lance lost.

I am falling.

I, the king, am lost.

The ground is hard and my horse when he lands is heavier still. His weight forces the breath from my lungs, and sickness swamps me. Prostrate, I stare at the sky, that pretty, bright blue sky, and then humiliation swamps me as my vision blurs.

I have lost. I am vanquished.

Someone is tugging at my helmet, and suddenly the frigid January air washes around my head.

"He is bleeding," someone calls. "The king is injured! Send for the physicians!"

Brandon is there, his blurred face white, a throbbing vein on his brow, his head haloed by cerulean blue sky.

"Henry ... Your Majesty!"

He shakes me, stares into my eyes, and I stare back but cannot make reply. My mouth will not obey my brain. I want to sit up and laugh, tell them all is well, that it will take more than a slight blow to fell their king for long, but my tongue is thick, too big for my mouth, and my head is swimming, and there is a devil of a pain gnashing at my leg.

Somewhere close, I can hear the painful grunts of my mount; his wind stolen, as is mine. I should have him destroyed for this.

They unbuckle my armour, their movements frantic, fumbling. Grandmother would say they were 'all fingers and thumbs.' Cold water is splashed on my face but still I do not move ... I cannot seem to.

I have heard of injuries where the victim is immobilised, lying abed for the rest of their short days – unmoving, unresponsive. That must not be the case now. I must take control of my wits. I must rediscover my speech and prevent them from bearing the news of this to Anne. She must not be told ... my son must be kept safe.

Suddenly, Norfolk is there. He pushes the other men aside, leans over me, his aged face creased with fear. He takes my hands and rubs them as if they are cold.

"Sire," he demands. "Sire, you must speak." He bends closer, pours his words directly into my ear. "The world is watching, Sire. You must rouse yourself."

He wants me to prove to the onlookers that I am not dead. It is important that I do so, but I can do nothing but stare at the sky. There are clouds now, white unthreatening wisps, like the heads of dandelion seed scattered on a summer pond. As I watch them float by, I hear laughter. It is Kate and Mary in the garden at Greenwich. I blink and try to call out to them, but then I remember that Kate is dead, and I have sent Mary far away.

I have another queen.

"He blinked!" someone cries. "I swear I saw him blink."

Norfolk scrambles to his feet, making way for the physicians who come puffing across the tiltyard, their long black robes flapping like the wings of carrion crows.

"I will inform the queen," he says, and my heart almost fails. I must stop him, I must stand up, I must call him back. The queen must not be told, my son … but although I make every effort, I do not move. I cannot move.

They carry me on a board back to the palace. It takes many men to bear me, and each swaying step increases the pain in my skull tenfold. If I were able, I'd lay about them with my knuckles, but I cannot even make a fist let alone follow up with a blow.

The palace ceilings pass above me. I had never noticed their adornment before, great carved oak beams, painted plaster, carved bosses gilded with cherubs. The world is reversed, and I now look up at all the things that usually look down upon me. I like not this reversal. I must get up; put an end to this fiasco. As we turn a corner into my privy apartments, I hear running footsteps.

"Henry!"

Damn. It is Anne. She runs headlong toward me, grabs my hand, her breath coming in short sharp gasps. They lower me to the floor, and she sprawls beside me, her face hanging above me, her eyes huge and dark with fear. I want to speak out, I must reassure her that I am well, that she need not worry, but instead I remain silent and cannot even return the pressure of her fervent fingers.

They lie me down upon my bed, remove my clothes, bathe my body, and pat me dry again before tucking warm furs up to my chin. Someone trickles water into my lips but I do not drink, I cannot seem to swallow. Moisture dribbles down my chin, collects in the creases of my neck. They dab me with handkerchiefs, cleanse the wound and bind my throbbing leg. All the while, their voices are low and apprehensive.

The queen remains at my side. I hear the anxiety in her voice, the questions she puts to the physicians, and I hear their replies – the prognosis is not good.

They say I may wake within the hour, or I may die before the night is out. I must not do that. I cannot leave the realm without an heir. There is only Elizabeth or Mary, or my unborn son. Had I the wit to wield a pen, I'd write that it must be Fitzroi. At least he is of an age to rule, and even if he lacks legitimacy, he is at least a male and of my blood.

I think it is much later, but I am not sure, it may just be moments that pass before I hear Jane's voice. She creeps into the room and asks the queen if there is anything she needs, if there is anything that she may do.

"You can pray, Strumpet," my gracious queen replies. "Pray that your leman lives, or I swear, his passing shall be swiftly followed by yours."

Jane makes no reply, but silently moves away. I hear the door close softly behind her and imagine her alone in the chapel, prettily praying for my life.

My fool, Will Somers, comes into view. He looms over me, his questioning eyes huge. He waves his rattle in my face, mutters something unintelligible before disappearing again.

At my side, Anne gnaws her nails and waits impatiently for me to stir. She is still beside me when darkness falls; I hear the logs in the grate crack and shift, sense that the candles have burnt low, and the fur beneath my chin irritates my nose.

I open my eyes.

"Anne?"

But she is gone, and so has the fool. Instead, a physician materialises at my side. With two fingers, he opens my eyelid wide, then drops his hand away as if it has been scalded.

"God be praised!" he exclaims. "The king lives! The king speaks!"

It seems my entire court has been slumbering about my chamber for it is suddenly full of men, full of activity. They cry out in joy, slap one another on the back, fall to their knees and give thanks at my recovery.

I am helped to sit, pillows are placed at my back, a cup held to my lips. Sweet, cold water – Adam's ale.

My mind begins to clear.

"We quite despaired of you, Sire." Brandon beams at me. His face is unwashed, and the marks of the recent joust are still upon him. Bryan is at his side, a hand upon his shoulder.

"And we are delighted at your recovery, Sire, I cannot express how much."

I push away the cup and glower at the assembly. Something is different. I can't quite place what it is, but the world seems … less bright. Perhaps, having looked death in the face, I am too aware that it will one day return and, when that day comes, I shall be granted no reprieve.

"Where is the queen?" I say, my voice thick and slow with misuse. "Why is she not here?"

They look shiftily, one to the other, as the chamber falls silent. There is a rustle of silk, the sound of a woman weeping. At length, Brandon rubs his nose.

"The queen is unwell, Your Majesty, and has taken to her chamber."

I know what is happening. They all know what is happening, but none dare speak of it. My head aches, my injured leg throbs, and my mind rages against fate. For five days, we wait while the queen bleeds, while her body expels my child, and eventually the physicians summon the courage to inform me that all hope is lost.

My son ... and it was a son ... has been taken, denied of a single living breath! It is *all* her fault. *Her* fault.

She lied to me. She has broken faith with the pledge she made to give me a son. I have gained nothing from her, but I have lost ... oh, so very much.

They wheel me to her chamber where, barely able look at her, I address my words to the far dark corner of her chamber, curt cruel words born of my own grief, my own disappointment. She holds out her arms that I might comfort her, but I cannot. A devil has taken up residence in my heart and I turn disgustedly away. Anne, the woman I turned the realm upside down to possess, has wounded me far worse than the lance, so I shun her and seek out softer, kinder arms.

February - March 1536

On her return to court, Anne is outwardly bright, showing an optimistic mask to the world. Her deathly pale face accentuates the darkness of her eyes, the redness of her lips, and her gaiety is unimpaired. I watch grimly as she pretends nothing is wrong. She may laugh, she may dance, she may drape her lithe body in bright fabrics, but that body is bone thin and when we are in private and she lets the charade drop, I see only hollow despair.

While Christendom laughs at my plight – *another lost son for the king of England,* they say – *another blow for the most virile, virtuous king of England* – I reluctantly take Anne back into my bed.

There is little joy in coupling with her now, but duty must be done. She is my wife and my queen, and she must give me a son. *I will have a son.*

The words play in my head as I ride her. I avert my eyes from her face and fix them on the bed hanging, plough her furrow as if my life depends upon it – which it does – and she writhes beneath me, grasping my ears, trying to make me love her, trying to lure me to look into her face, those eyes where sorcery lurks.

When I am done, I roll away and hurry to Jane. My body is tired, my mind is broken and all I crave is to sit at her feet with my head in her lap while she soothes my injured spirit.

But even she struggles to soothe this rage within me, which will never calm.

Anne and I argue over matters both huge and trivial. We are like two cocks in the pit, striking out, desperate to wound, to mortify, to destroy. Our hopes and promises are dust.

She forgets to close my birdcage and my finches escape, to flutter about the chamber like a handful of jewels before discovering the open window. I accuse her of intent, and we scream at each other, while the courtiers look on appalled. I hate her. I want to hurt her; I want to extinguish the fire in her that used to ignite mine. She spits cruelties at me, her eyes bright as daggers, her words as sharp, causing pain, drawing blood. I want to strike her but … chivalry prevents me, so I demean her instead.

While her household looks on in horror, I grab her wrist, drag her to our chamber and demand she be a wife to me. She does not demur but falls to her knees … where she belongs. And soon our anger switches to lust, and our lust evolves into a kind of sordid, twisted, Godless pleasure.

In the days that follow, our lovemaking is wild, unfettered by gentleness. As mad as I, she throws all caution aside and we rut with a desperation we've never before known. Soon, as if under some spell, I start to seek her out at all hours of the day, as well as the night.

She will give me a son.

And if, when I emerge from the queen's chamber, I happen to encounter Jane, I find it impossible to meet her eye, or seek her company later.

"Henry." Anne enters my chamber unceremoniously. She is already attired for bed, and I can tell straight away that she is agitated. Suffocating a sigh, I put down my pen and prepare for a tirade. "You must speak to Master Cromwell; he grows above himself."

"What has he done, now?"

I wave my hand to clear the room of servants and when the door is closed, she comes to sit on my knee, her arms snaking about my neck. There is no comfort in closeness to her now. I wince and urge her to move to my good leg.

"You know how I have been in discussion with the court of augmentations that rather than being shared among the nobility, the monasteries should become seats of learning and the revenue redirected into education and discovery rather than your coffers or those of Rome?"

I nod, watching a pulse beat at the base of her neck, my eyes trailing to her breasts. *Are they larger? Will she wince if I squeeze them? Is she perhaps already with child?*

Reaching out, I slide a hand into her loose gown, over her shift, and cup one, test the weight. She stops speaking.

"Henry! Are you listening?"

"Of course." I release her breast. "I think it's a good idea."

"Well. Your secretary disagrees. He thinks all revenue should revert to the Crown but ... you are more charitable than he. We could use the church wealth for good, it should not be squandered. It is important that we educate the people. We should keep those church rituals that convey deep meaning but educate the people so that they understand those meanings. The corrupt practices must be stopped: the selling of indulgences, the idea of purgatory, the ridiculous prayers to saints. It is our duty as King and Queen to free the people from superstition! Y-you agree with me, do you not?"

I make a swift calculation in my head. It is now early March, almost six weeks since she miscarried my son. I have visited her bed almost every night and even on some afternoons, yet still there are no signs she is pregnant. In truth, the constant strain is becoming tiresome, our nights together are exhausting, the continual need to implant a son on her robs the deed of all joy. I crave an end to it. I crave a son, and above all I crave some peace of mind.

She rises from my lap, spins on her heel and leans over me, a hand on each arm of my chair. In the candlelight, her features are sharp, her eyes piercing, the shadows from the flames making her appear older than her years.

"Henry! I am your queen. This is not the time for impartiality. You must help me in this. Your servant's teeth have become too sharp, and he must be muzzled."

"It is not so long since you and Cromwell were allies; now, because you've begun to argue, I am expected to choose whom to follow. I am the king, I follow no one."

She thumps the arms of my chair, stands up and begins to pace the floor, uttering a spate of angry words that I barely listen to. I am so tired of this. Tired of fighting, tired of turmoil.

Why can I not find peace?

And the face of Jane rises before me. Her gentle smile, her soft voice, her slightly off-key song, her sweet, womanly fragrance. I wonder where she is at this moment; perhaps I should seek her company again. She would welcome me, and I would not demand carnal pleasure but just the comfort of her friendship.

"You are not even listening! Your mind is far away!"

Anne's sharp tone brings me back to the matter in hand. I push myself up from my seat, reach for my stick and limp toward the door. As I pass her, I leave a kiss on her forehead.

"I am feeling unwell and must retire early. We can talk of this tomorrow when your temper has cooled."

As the door closes behind me, I hear something crash against the panelling and shatter to the floor. Another baluster jug, sacrificed at the altar of the queen's wrath. She would do well to remember who she is, how high I raised her and how easily I could send her back from whence she came. I should turn back and take her to task but instead, I shrug my shoulders, and go in search of peace.

As the weeks pass, the tension between us increases. Anne is high-handed, often cruel to her women, her opinions stated loudly regardless of whom they might injure or offend. I receive the worst of it, trapped in the middle of the constant battles between her and Cromwell. As often as I can, I creep off to be with Jane.

On one such wet afternoon, I am closeted with her in a small quiet chamber. I have persuaded her to put aside her sewing and sit upon my knee. She perches there warily, her face lowered, her cheeks enchantingly pink. With my forefinger beneath her chin, I am trying to tempt her to look into my face, but her reluctance is more arousing than eagerness would ever be. Suddenly, the curtain is thrown back and Anne is there, her face twisted and ferocious.

Jane leaps to her feet, falls to her knees, babbling as she begs Anne's forgiveness. The queen leans forward, the sinews in her neck straining, her face venomous.

"Strumpet!" she hisses and, spying the jewel I have lately fastened about Jane's neck, she tears it off, hurls it to the floor and crushes it beneath her heel. "And as for you, *Husband.*" She sneers. "Perhaps if you spent less energy dallying with whores you would have got a child upon me sooner. No wonder you struggle …"

She stops, belatedly realising the dangerous territory into which she has stepped.

"Get out!" she growls, her raised hand making Jane flinch away. Poor Jane flees and I want to follow her. I want to soothe her and reassure her of my love, but the queen must be placated. If she is with child, as she has hinted, she must remain calm.

"Anne." I breathe gently while fumbling around in my mind for some plausible excuse. "Come, let us not fight …"

She stares at me, her face twisted, her chest heaving. Her eyes narrow.

"I hate you, Henry. I would to God I had never laid eyes upon you … or you upon me. I rue the day you first looked upon me with desire. I should have married Harry Percy!"

She turns on her heel and leaves me.

But later, when I encounter her in the hall, it is as if the incident never happened. She is her brightest brilliant, gayest best as she dances with Norris, applauds Smeaton's newest refrain, and flirts ostentatiously with every gentleman in the room ... apart from Cromwell, of course, who watches darkly from a corner.

I raise my glass to him, and he returns the gesture, breaking off his conversation with Edward Seymour, Jane's brother, who, much to the queen's chagrin, is often at court these days. Anne complains he is a proud, unappealing fellow and I tend to agree. The company of the younger brother, Thomas, is far preferable for all his roguish ways.

The music ends, the courtiers applaud the queen's graceful performance and, during the lull that follows, a tide of chatter rises. Young pages weave in and out of the company bearing trays, offering sustenance. My own cup is half-full, but I have drunk little. My head is aching, as it often does of late, and I am resentful because my leg has still not healed, and I am unable to join the dance.

When the music begins again, Anne, not seeming to mind the lack of my company, takes to the floor with her brother, George. He enjoys attention as much as the queen, his clothes and bearing marking him out from other, lesser men. He cuts a fine figure; his limbs are long and whole, his face unblemished by trouble, his hair untroubled yet by grey.

The queen, meek for the purposes of the dance, is led well by her brother, who turns and spins her around, his hands light upon her torso. He bows and kisses her knuckles, and she laughs and simpers as if he were a lover.

It is all part of the game we play, the chivalry of love, the feigned desire, the poetry of hopeless adoration. Occasionally, the loving words become dangerous, especially when the game masks sincere desire but, of course, it isn't so with George and Anne for they are kin but ... what of the other men gathered?

I focus my attention on the rest of Anne's small band of courtiers. They are never far away, ever on hand should she desire an apple or a cup of wine. *How platonic are their real feelings? Do the playful words conceal some darker truth? What of Norris, and Brereton? What of ... any one of these men could harbour lecherous feelings for my wife.*

I look around the hall, scanning faces, noting the expressions of the gentlemen who watch in envy as my pretty queen cavorts with her brother. In each and every one of them, I see scarcely veiled lust.

<u>April 1536</u>

Rumours run around court about Jane, rumours that accuse her of being my mistress. I only wish it were so, but she is chaste, too chaste. I have to remind myself that this is a good thing, for virtue in a woman is paramount; I would not really have it any other way. Anne, of course, believing every word, is furious.

"I refuse to have her near me," she spits. "I can't imagine what you see in such an insipid, whey-faced whore."

Jane doesn't nag. The retort almost escapes my lips, but just in time I rein in the words, and my temper, for I am reluctant for yet another argument. I lie back in my seat, lace my fingers together, place them on my belly and listen to her continuing tirade.

"The whole court is laughing – not at me but you, for being duped by her lying cow's eyes."

"Then I will give leave for her to retire from court for a while, until the tongues have stopped wagging."

"Where will you send her? To one of your many houses, so that you may visit her at your leisure?"

"Don't be ridiculous, Anne. I am tired of this ..."

I wave my arm, lacking the words, wanting an end to it but, as ever, she is relentless once she has the rat between her teeth.

"Tired of this marriage? Of me?" She comes near, looms over me, and puts her nose close to mine. "I recall a time when you'd have given your life to possess me."

She clasps her hands together, pulls a moonstruck face and mocks me, mocks the love I once bore her. "*I crave you, Anne, my head is filled with you, night and day, I long for you! I must possess you, body and soul ...*' Well, your tune has certainly changed."

I refuse to argue. I merely blink at her while inside my fury is building to match hers. I watch as her rage increases. She straightens up, hands on hips.

"Will you not spar, Sir? Am I no longer even worthy of your displeasure?"

"Oh, do not mistake me, Madam, I am deeply displeased. I just choose not to take your bait."

"Such a clever fish," she mocks, her laughter high and erratic. "What a huge, clever cod-fish you are!"

If anyone hears her, I will be a laughingstock. My self control snaps and I lunge forward, grab her arm and twist it, our faces close, her lips – the lips I once longed to kiss – are so close I can taste her breath.

"Be careful, Anne, or you may go too far. Remember your betters ..."

"Oh, so you plan to treat me like you treated Catherine. You are going to shut me up in a dank castle in the wilds of the countryside so you can continue to dally with the Seymour bitch. And what then, my lord? Do you think you will ever know peace? Do you think you will ever forget me or the delight we have shared? For the sake of a fat, placid cow, you plan to forsake me? How long do you think it will last? You will rue the day, Henry. I promise you."

Her breath comes short and fast. Nose to nose, our hatred simmers, the tension between us stretching ever tighter. I want to hit her, I want to pull out her hair, I want to put my hands around that long, slender neck and throttle her, watch her eyes bulge as I squeeze the living breath from her.

Instead, I kiss her.

It is not a reconciliation. It is just me and Anne doing what we were born to do. We argue, we fuck, we grow cold again. It is like a dance that never ends, a dance that forces us into an endless circle, a dance that both satiates and destroys.

Jane flees from the queen's reach to her father's house until the rumours have abated, leaving me alone with Anne. I miss the sanctuary of Jane's quiet ministrations, her dull, gentle stories, her unswerving loyalty to the church. She abhors the religious changes that have been made but is careful not to apportion the blame to me. I soon gave up attempting to discuss such things with her as I so enjoy doing with Anne. Whereas Anne can debate until dawn on political matters, Jane resorts to tears for fear her opinions will offend me. If only I could find a woman somewhere in the middle. Someone gentle and wild, a paragon and a sinner, a saint and a harlot.

The queen and Cromwell continue to be at odds, and the court is watchful, everyone wary of speaking out too loudly in favour of either party before the winner is clear. As for me, I am sick of them all, tired of the endless rounds of debate, the rapidly increasing tension between members of the council. My head pounds, my leg throbs, and my heart aches.

Passion Sunday dawns bright, and since I've not seen the queen for two days, my spirit has calmed and, while I am dressed, I hum a tune I have been composing.

"What do you think, Norris, does that work?"

My attendants pause in their tasks to listen, heads on one side, faces open with interest. When I am done, they applaud, their flattering words bandying around the chamber.

Once my sleeves are tied, my doublet fastened, and the collar of the heavy coat artfully arranged, we quit the chamber and make for the chapel.

The congregation stands when I enter and I make my way to my seat, smiling benignly on the assembly as I pass between them. Even the queen, who has arrived before me, receives my gentlest greeting.

We pray and sing God's praises and then take our seats again and make ready to hear the sermon, which today is to be read by Anne's almoner, John Skip.

Filtered sunlight dapples the heads of the worshippers, and dances on the floor of the nave. Skip mounts the steps, clears his throat, and glances my way. As I wait for him to begin, I notice his face is paler than usual and there is a film of moisture on his upper lip. I hope he isn't sickening for something. I heard the sweating sickness is on the rise again. He moistens his lips and takes a deep breath before his words blast across the chapel.

"Which of you can convict me of sin …?" Startled, I fix my eye upon him, silently willing him not to continue, but he does not look my way. He dare not!

Knowing what is to come, I slide my gaze toward the queen, who sits with her chin high as if she has not a care in the world, but I am not blind. I know Anne well enough to recognise that there is defiance in every sinew. There is nothing I can do but listen as the words thundering from the pulpit condemn me and mine. If I rise and quit the chapel, my disapproval will only give the sermon credence and make tongues wag all the faster. But staying still and hearing it is akin to torture. Today, or tomorrow, or one day next week, I will have vengeance for this.

Skip hesitates, his voice lowering an octave as, with his courage waning, he continues.

"He became very un-noble and defamed himself sore by sensual and carnal appetite in taking of many wives and concubines …"

The inference is clear. My heartbeat increases, blood pounds in my ears. It is obvious Skip has the queen's endorsement; no one would dare compare me to Herod without it. If it were not so damaging, I would applaud the innovative way he deftly turns Cromwell into Haman, Herod's detested servant. So, the attack is not just against me but Cromwell too. I turn my head imperceptibly to gauge his response, but his face remains as bland as a bowl of cold pottage. But then my ear, keener than most, detects how Skip subtly misquotes the text to infer that Haman … or Cromwell, in his closure of the monasteries, is feathering his own nest.

In Skip's hands, Anne becomes Queen Esther – a blameless and a long-suffering victim. This is a deliberate comparison of a cruel king, an evil counsellor, and a virtuous queen. In the story, Esther begs of Herod: *"If I have found favour with the king, and if it pleases the king to grant my request, I ask that my life and the lives of my people will be spared."* But, by Christ, Anne will not be spared this, and neither will her almoner!

This is all Anne's doing. How dare she have me painted as a tyrant!

As soon as I may, I quit the chapel, snubbing all in my path. Managing to maintain an aura of calm, it is not until I reach the privacy of my chamber that I give vent to a rage so great that my fool takes refuge with the spaniels beneath the table.

The queen has gone too far; she has made a declaration of war against Cromwell and, even if she doesn't know it yet, against me - her king. That, without doubt, is treason.

May 1536

It takes several weeks to pass before the humiliating memory fades sufficiently to allow me to tolerate Anne's company without wanting to strike her. She didn't *mean* to shame me, I tell myself. Her intention was to warn Cromwell, to turn him from the path he is set on. Where once they were firm allies, Anne and Cromwell are now sworn enemies and I feel like the ball in a game of tennis, batted back and forth between them.

It makes my head sore. How I crave some peace.

But I am not allowed any. It is just a few days later that Cromwell seeks an audience. I am at my desk when he sidles through the door. I sigh, put down my pen and rest my forehead in my hand.

What now?

He moves quietly forward, makes his bow.

"Your Majesty, I trust you are well rested."

"I was, Cromwell, but I suspect that now you are here, my peace of mind will soon be spoiled."

He is silent for a while before he makes a whispered reply.

"Quite possibly, Your Majesty."

He looks at the ceiling.

"Well, what is it? I have other business to attend to this morning."

He clears his throat. "I suspect treason, Your Majesty … in your very court."

My head jerks up. The word 'treason' is always guaranteed to strike fear into my soul.

"What treason? Who?"

He moves closer, bends over the table, his voice lowering so that his news is heard by me alone.

"I have not yet concluded my investigation into the matter, Your Majesty, but what I have so far discovered prompts me to beg your leave to continue …"

"What do you mean, 'beg my leave?' When have you ever required my permission to seek out traitors?"

He coughs nervously. "The matter concerns men close to you and may also involve …" he hesitates, wets his lips, "… the queen."

I jolt so violently that something cracks in my neck. I put up a hand, try to massage the pain away.

"What do you mean? Be specific, man!"

"I am not yet certain, but it seems some indiscretions may have occurred …"

"Indiscretions? Between whom? Speak plainly."

"… B-between the queen and certain members of your court."

My heart sets up a loud and steady thump, my ears begin to ring, and the world around me is suddenly surreal. Perhaps I am asleep and dreaming. This cannot be real. I cannot be sitting here while my chief minister informs me that I am made a cuckold. There must be a mistake, but he cannot look me in the eye. He fiddles with the papers on the desk, forms them into a pile, picks them up again and squints toward the candle.

"Which members?"

He looks sheepish. Lifts his arms and drops them again. A few pieces of parchment float to the floor but he makes no move to retrieve them.

"Young Smeaton, perhaps ... Norris."

"NORRIS?"

He inclines his head, eyes closed as if he is too pained to look at me. I plump down into my chair; stare distractedly at the scattered pens, the sealing wax, and leaves of paper.

This cannot be true. Anne would not dally. She may resent my feelings for Jane, but she would not betray me. *And Norris?* He is an honest fellow. He is my friend, one of my closest companions ... he would not. Anne would not ... Smeaton? That dark-eyed boy? I remember the lovelorn looks he cast in the queen's direction. How I joked with Anne, the silly nickname she gave him, Smeaton the Smitten. I recall how she threw back her head and mocked his devotion when all the time she ... she was really ... laughing at me.

Suddenly hot, I fumble for my kerchief and mop my forehead. This is not true. This cannot be true. I feel sick. My heart leaps; my breath comes quick and painfully. I drop my head, put a hand to my face and squeeze the bridge of my nose, forcing myself to think.

What if it is true? What if Anne has made a cuckold of me? What if every man in Christendom knows of it and is laughing? My fury dissolves into shame, and then to grief.

Anne, Anne, my Anne, have you truly done this thing? Have you turned me into a laughingstock? To my dismay, a tear rolls down my nose and falls onto my hand. I dash it away before Cromwell has time to see. I clear my throat but when I speak my voice betrays me, my words are husky with sorrow. Grief and rage is strangling me.

"Who else knows of this?"

"Oh, nobody, Your Majesty. I have been discreet in my enquiries so far."

"You must discover more, Cromwell. I need proof. I need witnesses. I need names, dates, and times. When it happened, where it happened as well as with whom. And I need it promptly."

He bows again, backs from the chamber and softly closes the door, leaving me alone with my tortuous thoughts – thoughts that scream in the solitary silence. I fall back in my seat, cover my face with my hands and weep.

I weep for so long that the afternoon passes into evening. When they come to close the shutters and light the torches, I send them away. I sink my head back into my hands and let despair engulf me again. How can this be true? How can I have spent so long in love with a woman only to discover I know her not at all?

I take out a kerchief, mop my wet face and frown. In the stillness of the chamber something drops to the floor, something small, like a pin that bounces once, twice, thrice … I raise my head, turn slowly and peer into the shadow.

Cut and Ball are curled near the cold hearth, their heads tucked beneath their tails, sleeping blissfully, unaware of my deep grief. Beside them, I notice another shade, a larger darker grey lump indistinguishable in the bad light. As I try to determine what it is, the shape moves, metamorphoses into a figure. I can clearly see an arm, a head. I spring from my seat.

"Who is it? What are you doing here?"

I grab the single candle, almost burned out on my desk, and thrust the puny light into the corner. Cut and Ball rouse themselves, their tails beating the floor. "Who are you?" I shout again, and the guards come crashing belatedly through the door.

I stand back and allow them to do their duty. The fellow who has been crouching in the corner begins to cry, loud outraged bellows of terror. As they drag him into the light, he blinks at me. Wide, round eyes, gaping mouth. My body deflates with relief. I hold up a hand.

"Hold!" I command. "Leave him go. It is a simple mistake. It is only Will."

They back off warily while my fool crouches, shamefaced and afraid, at my feet.

"There's nothing to be afraid of, Will," I say. "I mistook you for an assassin."

He looks hangdog, unsure if he can trust the guards not to fall upon him again. I wave them from the room.

"Leave us, we will be fine," I say, and they troop out, swords clattering, and leave me alone with my fool. Two fools together, I think wryly as I pour us each a cup of wine.

Will Somers has been at court for a while now. He is an amusing addition to the entertainments and has formed an attachment to my spaniels, often joining them on their walks about the castle grounds. This morning ... was it truly only this morning? So much has happened since ... he was throwing sticks for them. I recall at one point laughing when he took one in his own mouth and played tug of war with Ball.

"Have you been here all day? You must be starved."

He eyes the plate of wafers on my desk, and I reach out and offer him one. He takes it warily, shovels it into his mouth, crumbs catching in his beard and falling to his green coat.

If he has hidden with the dogs at the hearth all day, he will have heard everything, witnessed the worst moment of my life. The only comfort I can find in this is that if he speaks of it, nobody at court will take it seriously. If he is renowned for anything, it is speaking nonsense.

I slump back in my seat and realise that perhaps some of the hollowness I am suffering could be due to hunger. I've not eaten since breaking my fast just after dawn. I call for my servant and when he pokes his head warily around the door, I send him for food.

"Bring enough for two," I add. "My companion here is as hungry as I."

And so, on the darkest evening of my life, I dine in comfort with the court fool. He is quiet at first but, as his belly fills and his wine cup empties, he speaks of this and that. His words are gentle, humdrum; there is no intrigue, no spite, no politics, no hostility. He tells me of a rabbit he saw in the meadow, the way the tassels on the drapery remind him of Cut and Ball's tails. He is not an idiot, not even a fool. He is a simple man, free of earthly care. His life is soft, warm, full of laughter and fun, light and joy. As I listen to his chatter, I consider the differences between me and Will Somers, and it becomes very clear which of us is the bigger fool.

When he has eaten his fill, he stands up, wipes his hands on his velvet coat and bows to me.

"Thank you for the supper, Your Majesty," he says, with a sweeping bow that would have graced the finest courtier. "I like those tarts."

He points to a half empty plate and, taking the hint, I reach out and hand him two, which he places carefully in his pocket.

"Thank you for joining me," I reply. "We must dine together more often."

And with a little skip of happiness, he quits the chamber and leaves me with my demons.

It all happens so fast. Within a week, Cromwell is back with news that Smeaton has confessed to carnal knowledge of the queen. Bile swirls in my gut. My head swims. *How could she do such a thing?* I have been honest and faithful to her since the first day I saw her, and all that time she has been deceiving me. How? Why? For how long? Can I even be certain that Elizabeth is mine?

To my shame, Cromwell bears witness to my disintegration. I raise a dread face to his, and I find compassion, regret and sorrow in his eyes. He is an honest man, for all his humble beginnings, I must not forget that. It takes a brave soul to bring such news to a king. I must ensure he is rewarded.

"What now?" I ask, our roles reversed as he becomes the master and I the servant. "What now must be done?"

He clears his throat, speaks patiently, carefully, as if to a child.

"Smeaton has implicated several others in the crimes against Your Majesty. I ask your leave to question them next."

"Who?" My voice breaks, the shards of my heart and my pride scattering to the floor.

"Norris, as I mentioned before. Brereton, Weston … Rochford."

"Rochford! Don't be a fool, man. Rochford is her brother … it isn't …"

But I do not finish the sentence; of course, it is possible. If a woman is depraved enough to sleep with half my court, it is but a short step further to commit incest.

Tears burn like hot wax down my cheeks.

"How can I have been so blind, Cromwell? I thought she loved me, I thought her honest, I thought her pure. When I first lay with her, I swear she was …"

But was she? Is it possible that Anne was no virgin when I first took her to my bed? When we were wed, was I taking on another man's leavings? She made me wait so long yet she spent her youth in France, at the court of that vile lecher, Francis. It is common knowledge that the French king had her sister, Mary, as his concubine, why not Anne too? Oh no, not Anne! Not my Anne!

It hurts to breathe; I cannot fill my lungs. I feel my head is going to explode.

They've taken Wyatt now, and Bryan too. Men I have known for years, men I've sparred with, drunk with, hunted with.

My friends.

When I see their names, scrawled alongside the other traitors, I think of them enjoying my wife, imagine her taking lascivious pleasure with them. Laughing at me! I cannot stop the tears. I lay my head on the desk and while I give vent to grief, Cromwell slips discreetly away.

I cannot let the world see how broken I am. Nobody must know that my heart, my pride, is in tatters. I am the King of England! I cannot shut myself away. Instead, I order up a feast, and call for music … and if I cannot find the will to dance, I place the blame on my damaged leg, not my spirits.

No man shall ever guess that I've been broken by something as commonplace as the betrayal of my wife.

With my companions, my *friends*, incarcerated in the Tower, I am attended by strangers. They don't know how I like things to be done. They tie my laces crooked, they mix my drinks to their taste, not mine, they do not instantly understand my jokes. They forget to laugh, they forget to praise my well-turned leg, the glory of my new coat, the perfect setting of a new ring. There is not a soul in the palace who understands or knows me as my old friends did; there are only newcomers, interlopers.

This new state of affairs is most displeasing. My heart is broken, my pride is torn, and my bed is empty.

I do not see Anne again. I try not to think of her in the Tower. I cannot bear it. I cannot tolerate the thought of it. I dare say she laments of her sins, and she will hope for mercy, but she will come to understand that she must die.

There is nothing that can save her. I shut out her face. I close my mind to the memory of our love and concentrate upon destroying her.

I hone my attention on every step of the process. I must know about the trial, the building of the scaffold, the manner in which the convicted are to die. The men, those *traitors*, will be beheaded, and the only honour the whore will be granted is being the last to die. Let her watch her lovers suffer and witness the manner of death that she too will shortly face.

But, latterly, as the fact of her death becomes inevitable, I falter. I cannot bear to have her lovely head hacked from her shoulders, so I show mercy and send to France for an executioner skilled with the sword. Her past service to the crown deserves that at least.

I am close to panic by the time her execution draws near, so I send for Jane to comfort me. I provide her with lodging on the Strand, a mile or so from Whitehall that I might visit discreetly and at my leisure. No matter how much pain it inflicts on me, I must close my mind to Anne.

She was yesterday. That day is done.

Jane, housed in splendour as would befit a queen, is nervous when I visit her. She allows me to hold her hand but seems to take no pleasure in it. I am longing for her to show some passion; I want to feel her arms about me. I want to throw convention to the wind but, try as I might to seduce her, she clings to her chastity like a drowning woman to a branch.

"It is not long, Sire, before you take me as your wife, and I must come to our marriage bed with my chastity intact."

I cannot argue. I applaud her virtue but ... I need her. I need the release. I need a distraction from the horror that has taken hold of my court. Only she can obliterate the knowledge of what is happening to Anne. Sometimes, I am afraid that if someone does not stop me, I will scream to the rooftops for someone to halt the executioner.

So many times before I have forgiven Anne her faults and taken her back, but now I cannot. Yet my bed is empty, and my heart is so sore. I am starved of affection.

"We will be married the instant we can," I say, pawing at Jane's hands, kissing her soft, cool cheek. She lifts her shoulder, glances coyly up at me, and then casts her gaze downward again.

"I pray it is soon, Sire. I could swoon from wanting you and wish to make you happy."

But she speaks without passion and I suspect she has been schooled to say such things. I cling to her emotionless words.

"You could make me happy now, Jane. It would be so easy. I will be so gentle ..."

I cup her breast, squeezing softly, although I can feel nothing through the thick brocade of her gown. She looks away, her throat working as if she would weep, and I whip my hand away again.

"Oh, Jane, do not cry. I am sorry. I will wait."

The world seems empty and hollow now. It is only a matter of weeks since Cromwell brought me word of Anne's infidelity yet already the deed is done. She is gone. Dead, and half my court gone with her. Only Bryan and Wyatt were found to be free of guilt. I thank God for their loyalty, thank God they managed to resist her wiles. It is hard to believe. The whole sorry affair seems like a nightmare now. Her lovely head has been parted from her luscious body and she has gone from

106

this world, from my court, from my bed, yet ... still she lingers. She haunts my dreams, taunts me with her open arms, her pleading eyes, her severed neck. The blood.

Oftentimes, when I am alone, I think I hear her laughter; a quick footstep makes me look up, expecting her to burst through the door. If I hear a strain of music we once danced to, my heart breaks open and I am lost again.

I cling to Jane but my wife, my new queen, is disgruntled when at the height of our passion, I call out my dead wife's name instead.

June 1536

I scan the contents of the letter, skimming over words and phrases.

Most humbly prostrate before the feet of your most excellent majesty, your most humble, so faithful and obedient subject, who has so extremely offended your most gracious highness that my heavy and fearful heart dare not presume to call you father, deserving of nothing from your majesty, save that the kindness of your most blessed nature does surmount all evils, offences and trespasses, and is ever merciful and ready to accept the penitent calling for grace, at any fitting time.

I let the letter drop.

"At last, Cromwell! She capitulates at last."

"I sometimes doubted this day would ever come, Your Majesty."

I offer him a cup, pick up my own and we drink deeply. Mary is as stubborn as her mother, but I have finally won. At last, she has acknowledged that the marriage between Kate and I was no marriage and conceded that she is not my legitimate daughter. Of course, it comes a little late now that Elizabeth is named a bastard too. Cromwell begins to tidy up the parchments that are scattered on the table.

"Will you summon her back to court, Your Majesty?"

I rub my chin, the fine hair bristling under my fingertips.

107

"I will, Cromwell, but first she should write to the queen, and do her honour as her mother. On her return, Mary will rank second only to the queen and there must be no animosity between them."

"I don't think you need worry on that score, Your Majesty. Queen Jane was always a friend to the Dowager … Princess of Wales."

He nearly slipped and called her dowager queen and is aware that I noted his near blunder. We exchange wry smiles, but I can forgive him the slip since I sometimes make the same mistake.

"Once she has made overtures of friendship to the queen, we will be happy to welcome Mary back to court. See the arrangements are made."

I sense the battle with Mary is almost done and realise I have Norfolk to thank for it. Cromwell's soft methods of persuasion proved useless and somehow, it was Norfolk who managed to undermine her protest and persuade her to submit.

Now that I reflect on it, it is a shame it was ever necessary to cast Mary off. Had her mother only bowed down gracefully and retired from public life, our relationship would have flourished. I could have embraced Kate as a sister and treated Mary in a similar regard to that which Fitzroi enjoys. But, unfortunately, I missed the larger part of her adolescence, and she is a grown woman now. This could, of course, prove useful to me for, legitimate or not, as my daughter she will still attract an advantageous match.

I must give the matter further thought.

"Oh, Henry, I am so pleased!"

The queen claps her hands and smiles broadly when I relay the news of Mary's acquiescence. Somers leaps up and begins clapping and cavorting too, although he has no idea what has made the queen so happy.

Jane has long been soliciting for Mary's return to court. If it were up to Jane, she would be fully reinstated and given back her title of 'princess.' Foolish, doting woman; she doesn't realise that such a move would place my eldest daughter before any daughter Jane may yet bear. Although she could, of course, never supplant a son.

My daughter is welcome to return to us, for as long as she behaves, and it will be good for Jane to have a friend of near status. As for Elizabeth, who now shares Mary's illegitimate status, Jane can argue all she likes for her return.

I am not yet ready for that.

Elizabeth unsettles me. Her dark Boleyn stare seems all-knowing but, secretly, beyond all things, I fear that one day I will look upon her and see a likeness to Brereton or Norris, or Weston or Smeaton or, God forbid, even George.

I shake my head to exorcise the ill thoughts that haunt me and grope for Jane's hand.

"Perhaps, my dear." I say, when she requests yet again for my daughter to be allowed to return. "We shall see and, all being well, she can join us at court for Christmas this year."

"Christmas?" Will pops his head from beneath the table where he has been helping the dogs find scraps. "I like Christmas; is it soon?"

"Only six or seven months away, Will," I laugh. "The time will pass before we know it."

July 1536

But kings have no need to wait for December to make merry and, for a while, the court becomes gay again. There are feasts and jousts, entertainers from the courts of Europe, but there are shadows too. Cromwell keeps me informed of the mood of the people and I am surprised by reports of those who question the speed with which I married Jane. *Would they deny their king's happiness? Have I not suffered enough? Do they not realise the importance of begetting an heir?*

Although I admit it to no one, I am beginning to feel my age, my leg causes me constant pain, and since I can no longer hunt or joust as often or for as long as I used to, I am growing fat. Thankfully, the extra weight becomes me well and I still cut a fine figure in my court clothes. I have noticed the male courtiers have taken to wearing padding beneath their doublets, and wires in their sleeves to give the appearance that they are as well built as I.

Jane shares my love of finery, and her wardrobe accounts are higher than either Anne's or Kate's ever were. But although I should urge her to show some economy, I can deny her nothing. In fact, I appreciate how her rather plain dumpy figure is enhanced by the velvets and silks she favours.

While the court is brightened by the fashion for vibrantly hued fabric, there have been more unwelcome changes to women's wardrobes. I have noticed their upper bosom is modestly covered now, and their hair, which was once visible under the French style of cap, is now hidden beneath the ugly gabled style that Kate once favoured.

I imagine Jane strives to be the opposite of Anne in every way, thank Heaven, or perhaps she believes the style is more personally becoming to her broader features.

Whatever the reason behind these recent fashion changes, my new queen is compliant to my wishes where her predecessor was stubborn, she is gentle where Anne was sharp, but she has no humour and is very little fun. She often fails to laugh at my jokes, she is earnest when I wish to be gay, and in bed, although she is submissive, she is greatly lacking in vigour. Sometimes I feel it would be easier to roll over and sleep than go to the effort of getting a son on her, but I know my duty.

Her household is expanding though, and it is a joy to see so many new young faces. There are some women I have not met before; young girls whose beauty far outshines the queen's. So much so that when I look around the hall, I wonder if I was hasty in wedding Jane, for her allure has lessened now I no longer require a salve to Anne's sting.

Perhaps I should have sought a younger wife, a girl in her teens with many childbearing years ahead but ... 'tis done now. Jane is good, at least. She is virtuous, pious, and honest, and the shirts she embellishes for me are almost as good as those Kate made. On the nights that I sleep alone, I rest easy in my bed, confident that she is not sporting with other men.

In marrying Jane, I have not only done her the honour of making her queen but have heaped honours on her family. Her father is ailing but her elder brother, Edward, a dry sort of fellow, is now a Viscount, and I have engaged the younger of the brothers, Thomas, as a gentleman of the privy chamber. His presence is uplifting for he is a fun-loving fellow of ready wit and a welcome addition to my household. Once his sister has given me a son, I will raise him further still.

I ease my leg onto a stool and lie back in the chair. Outside, the day is bright, and I wish I could ride out with the hunt as I used to. Sometimes, I fear I will never mount a horse again. Even to walk my dogs on the heath would make a welcome change to these four walls. When I complain of it, Jane chides me gently.

"We must give thanks that Your Majesty survived such a nasty fall," she says, earnestly patting my knee. "I pray for your full recovery every day."

She really is as dull as ditch water. I smile emptily, cover her hand with mine, and wonder if she is yet with child. Her cheeks are pale, but they are ever so. I always knew the instant Kate or Anne had conceived; Kate would vomit at the slightest suggestion of food and Anne's body would change, her breasts would swell, her face would become fuller. Although I see no such indication in Jane, I open my mouth to ask her anyway, but my words are forestalled when the door opens, and Cromwell is announced.

"Your Majesty …" He pauses, looks about the chamber. "Oh, I had expected Norfolk would be in attendance on you."

"Well, he isn't here, Cromwell. Unless you suspect he is hiding behind the draperies with Somers." I laugh and wave my arm to where the fool has concealed himself behind the great tapestries that line the walls. He joins me while Jane looks uncertain; she glances about as if to check that Norfolk isn't lurking there in truth. I choose not to draw attention to her lack of wit.

"What can I do for you? Or were you in search only of my lord of Norfolk?"

"I have some news, Your Majesty, that I felt the duke and I should deliver jointly."

Suspicion prickles at the back of my neck. I sense the news is not good. Norfolk and Cromwell are not friends, they never have been. Norfolk resents my secretary as an upstart, and Cromwell regards him as … well, he hasn't confided his feelings on the matter to me, but it is clear the dislike is mutual. If the two are working in tandem, it can only be ill news. I release Jane's hand and sit up, lift my leg from the stool, and wince as my foot touches the ground.

"What has happened?"

Cromwell's chest expands as he draws in breath and opens his hands, palms upward.

"Your Majesty will recall that your son, the Duke of Richmond, was ailing when you saw him last?"

"Yes, yes. I trust he is better …"

It is not a question; it is more of a demand. Fitzroi is dear to my heart.

"He has taken a turn for the worse, Your Majesty. We … Norfolk and I … thought you might like to visit …"

It is an inclement day and, suddenly chilled, I draw my gown closer about my shoulders, and Jane's fingers tighten about mine. I look into Cromwell's dark, unfathomable eyes.

"Is … is he dying?"

I speak quietly, unwilling to hear the answer. I want him to laugh and deny it. I want him to tell me it is all a misunderstanding, that the boy is well, he is merely suffering from a passing malady and there is nothing for which to be concerned.

"I am afraid the … the physicians fear that may be so, Your Majesty."

For once, Cromwell lets his feelings show and I see the unshrouded pity in his eyes. He knows what it is to lose a child.

I want to weep but I do not. I want to fall to my knees and curse God for depriving me of my only son … if Jane fails to give me a legitimate heir then, bastard or not, Fitzroi would have been the one chosen to follow me, but perhaps King

Henry IX is not meant to be. It seems many of my hopes and dreams will never come to pass.

So much wasted effort. The money, the titles, the education, the hope that I have poured into him. I remember the pleasure of his begetting. How effortlessly I planted my seed into the womb of his plump, young mother, and how easily she nurtured that seed and gave me a male child. The simple task of reproduction that has since become so very hard.

"Bessie," I say. "She has been informed?"

"I understand that his mother is with him."

Bessie has been twice married and is now the mother to many sons. Perhaps I would have done better to have wedded her instead of Anne, and all this could have been avoided. She is handsome still, they say.

"Does Your Majesty wish to …?"

I wave him away.

"I will think on it, Cromwell. Not today … I don't feel up to it today."

I remember when my father died. I waited for a summons, expected him to ask for me so he could tell me of his pride in me, his conviction that I would be a good king. I sat near his chamber, watching as physicians, privy councillors, and servants went in and out. His summons never came, and even when I was allowed to creep in and sit beside grandmother while the last rites were read and we watched as he breathed his last, he never spoke.

He never asked for me.

I needed to hear that I had mattered to him, that I was mistaken in my belief that I ranked a poor second to Arthur in the king's affection. I needed him to tell me I would make a successful monarch; that he was proud of me.

Fitzroi and I have never been close. I have honoured him, kept him clothed and well housed. Despite his bastardy, I have raised him, given him titles; Duke of Richmond and Somerset, made him the highest in the land as are his offices but … I do not *know* him.

Other men sport with their sons, they take pride in their achievements and when they grow to a man's estate, they offer one another mutual support, camaraderie. I have never known how to do that with my son. Perhaps, if I go to him now, I can speak to him of his importance to me, his significance to the realm. I never even told him of my plan to name him my heir.

There have been other bastards over the years, of course, but none that I've acknowledged. When Fitzroi was born, I was young and so proud to have sired a living son that I wanted the fact proclaimed across the land. I soon learned that bastard sons prove just as expensive as legitimate offspring, and my purse was not deep enough to finance more. So, although I watch them and wonder about them from a distance, and regret the boys I've sired on other women, I lay no claim to them.

Fitzroi will be a great loss to us, to England. Tears sting my eyes. Surreptitiously, I wipe them away and, when Jane notices my grief and begins to fuss, I snatch my hand away.

There are some things a man must face alone.

I reach for my stick, limp across the chamber and lay a hand on Cromwell's shoulder.

"Should I visit him, Cromwell? Would that be fitting ... he is not ... contagious?"

"We believe not. I understand Norfolk has been with him. Perhaps he could accompany you, Sire."

Norfolk. He will be as irked about my son's death as I. It is only a few years since he contrived a marriage between Fitzroi and his daughter, Mary. The union with my blood promised to be advantageous for the whole Howard family. He will fret at the severance, the loss of future opportunity.

A thought occurs.

"Cromwell, the marriage between my son and Mary Howard, it remained unconsummated?"

"It did, Sire, so I believe."

His quick mind follows my line of thought, and he nods discreetly.

"I will ensure the lands and titles are returned to the crown, Sire. A wife who was no wife should receive no widow's entitlement."

I wave him away and he begins to back toward the door.

"Oh, Cromwell …" He halts and waits for my words.

"I think I would like to visit and make my farewell to Fitzroi, after all. Arrange it, would you, but keep the matter quiet, and inform Norfolk that he is to accompany me."

But … it is too late. Before the visit can be arranged, word comes that Fitzroi has passed. I am too late to make amends. Too late to say goodbye. That tiny boy, who pissed on my jerkin at our first meeting, is no more and I am left with no son, no heir, not even a bastard.

Failure sits heavily on my shoulders, but I conceal it as I always do. There is no need for them to know how deeply I am affected, they'd only fuss, but Fitzroi's passing haunts me. His death feels like a betrayal.

For seventeen years, he has been the only living proof of my virility, the reassurance that I do have the capacity to breed a son. Now, I have no son, no legitimate heir, and my wife is … not as young as she could be.

I have regretted more than once not choosing a bride more carefully. I did not take time to consider every avenue. Had I not been in such need of comfort, and had she not been there waiting with her arms outstretched, it is very likely I would never have taken refuge there. But it is too late for regret. The union is consummated; I cannot seek an annulment now.

She must give me a son! And fast!

Fitzroi's death has left more than a hole in my heart; it has created a huge void in the country. He was the highest-ranking peer in the land; the Duke of Richmond and Somerset, a knight of the garter, Lord High Admiral of England, Lord lieutenant of Ireland, Warden of the Cinque ports, Constable of Dover Castle, Lord President of the council of the North,

Warden of the Marches, and Chamberlain of Chester and North Wales … the list is long.

They were heavy mantles for a feeble seventeen-year-old boy, and all those positions must now be refilled. His properties must be reassigned; his huge retinue must be found employment elsewhere, his servants and tenants re-

The doors are thrown open and Norfolk enters. He hesitates when he notices my dishevelled hair, my wet cheeks …

"Your Majesty. I - I apologise for the intrusion. I thought you were waiting for me. I will return later …"

Somers, having no liking for Norfolk, rises from his seat at the hearth and creeps from the room. I swipe the tears from my face and wave him forward.

"No matter, Norfolk. I confess I am feeling glum and could do with the company. Besides, there are matters to be discussed."

He gives a wry smile and takes the proffered seat, clears his throat, and places a hand on each knee.

"He will be greatly missed, Sire. My daughter is distraught."

I glance up at him. How distraught can an un-bedded woman be? She hasn't lost anything of value, she still has her virtue, there are no offspring to worry about, and she is young enough to remarry. Her grief will be short lived. Her loss is nothing compared to mine!

But I do not say these things aloud.

"Bury him quietly, Norfolk."

"Your Majesty?"

He leans forward in his seat, a hand behind his ear to indicate he has not caught my words.

"Bury him quietly, at Thetford. I cannot face a great ceremonial funeral at this time. See it is done decently and discreetly."

He looks puzzled. I daresay he'd been expecting high ceremony. He'd have enjoyed the House of Norfolk at the hub of public interest, but he was *my* son, not Norfolk's. It shall be

done my way. The duke cannot argue, not with me. He bows his head.

"I will see that it is done, Your Majesty, and should I order mourning for the household?"

I stare at him. I do not care. I just want it to be over.

I spend too much time alone, too much thinking, and my thoughts are often unbearable. The tribulations the good Lord heaps upon me are too heavy. I want to close my eyes and forget. I crave a deep dreamless sleep; I want to wake up in a new dawn, into a day where I am young again, where I am free of bodily pain, free of heartache, free of troubles and surrounded by small, healthy sons.

Later that evening, although my leg is throbbing, I visit the queen in her chamber. I informed her earlier that I was coming so she is ready for me. When her women leave us, they take Will Somers with them, linking both his arms with theirs and carrying him away, his feet pedalling when he resists.

Jane's smile is soft and welcoming; she strokes and soothes and whispers as I have taught her. When I begin to strip off her clothes, she stands compliant. I push her to the bed, climb upon her but …

I roll back on the mattress, pain shooting through my thigh. "God's curses on this leg!"

"Don't worry, Henry. I shall fetch your physician …"

"No, no, wait."

I grab her arm as she begins to slide from the bed, pull her against me.

"You must do it, Jane."

"I must do … what?"

"For God's sake, woman." I try not to speak though gritted teeth. "It will be more comfortable if you mount me."

Even the ill light from the candles does not disguise her blushes when she sees I am in earnest. She pales just as quickly, as if I've asked her to dance naked before the court. Awkwardly, she slides her knee across me, sits upright and turns her face to the wall as I position myself inside. I pant and sweat until the pain passes.

"Now, you must wriggle and bounce a bit."

I slap her thigh encouragingly and, biting down upon her lower lip, she does as she is bid. I squint up at her and her obvious distaste for the task extinguishes every ounce of my arousal.

Even when I was in full health, Anne would ride me like this; just for the fun of it, she'd pretend I was her palfrey, and she was in pursuit of a hind. She'd lay about me with an imaginary whip. I can see her now, teeth bared, her hair streaming like serpents across her bare bouncing breasts.

"Faster, Henry, faster!" she'd cry, and we'd pound away together until we were both spent. Jane melts away and Anne takes her place in my head. I close my eyes, reach out for her breasts but find Jane's instead, which are larger and less firm than Anne's. I close my eyes tighter.

"Faster," I say, "harder!" and with a whimper, she obeys, her breasts bouncing in my hands, her bare buttocks slapping against my thighs.

Anne! Anne! Her name resounds in my mind, her scent fills my nose. I grab her hair and pull her closer, cover her mouth with mine, my tongue snaking with hers, my hands clenching tight as I fire my seed.

"Anne …"

Jane sits up, draws her hand across her wet mouth, and uncouples us before falling on the bed beside me. From the corner of the chamber, I hear a small sound, a trickle of merriment. I turn toward it. Anne is fading now but before she goes, she places two hands about her neck and laughs.

"Comfort me, Jane."

"What, again, my lord?"

"No, no. Just let me lay my head against you …"

She is propped up on pillows while I snuggle into the crook of her arm, relish the softness of her breast beneath my cheek, and close my eyes. I turn from the memories of Anne and urge Jane to stroke my shoulder. I cling to her, relishing the beat of her living heart, the soft hush of her breath as her chest rises and falls.

"Henry, do you think she cursed him?"

I am jerked instantly from the brink of peace. I sit up, peer at her through the gloom.

"Who? What do you mean?"

She frowns, shakes her head.

"Forgive me. I was thinking aloud."

"You meant Anne, I suppose … you think she cursed my only son from the scaffold?"

"Well, he was there, wasn't he? Didn't you send him to witness her death?"

Her voice has dropped to a whisper, making the hair prickle on the back of my neck. Fitzroi was there, he did witness Anne's death, but … is that possible? Could the condemned cast some sort of spell on the living? *Would* she?

I think of Anne, her temper, quick and lethal, and the almost instant contrition that usually followed. Perhaps Jane is right and in the moment before death she was angry enough to bite me in the heel before she died, and was not given the time to retract it.

No, no – she didn't. This is just some ridiculous idea of Jane's, dreamed up in the darkest hour of the night. I raise my head to look at her. Her face gleams pale in the dim light and fear is written large across her features. Fear of what?

"You never liked the queen, did you, Jane?"

She starts, stares at me for a moment before shaking her head, just once.

"She was difficult to like. I misliked her horrible little dog too."

"Purkoy?" I scramble up in bed, dragging the covers with me, exposing her nakedness. "You mean you … you didn't hurt him, did you?"

"Oh no, Sire! I didn't mean that. I was just remembering the difficulties of being in her household, especially once she knew you had a care for me. She used to make me take Purkoy outside every hour on the hour, and he'd nip at my ankles. It was as if she'd trained him to do so. Once, he drew blood and the queen just laughed when she saw the wound. She said it served me right and made a fuss of the dog, said he was a good judge of character."

I smile despite myself. I can see Anne doing that. Suddenly, it is as if she is there before me, her eyes full of mischief. Open honest spite, that was Anne's weapon, she'd never be underhanded enough to curse my son …even if she were capable of it.

Choosing not to pursue the matter, I shake my head to rid myself of Anne, but she clings like a canker to my mind.

I give the approximation of a laugh.

"He used to nip me too if he got the chance. He was quite jealous of his mistress."

"So was I," Jane says, as she snuggles beside me again. We lie nose to nose, and I watch as her eyes grow heavier, and her breathing slows. Once she is snoring gently, I slide from the bed and stand at the window. Alone in the dark, I think of the women I've known. I think of my mistresses, my wives. I think of Kate, and of Anne, of the promises that were broken, the betrayal of my friends. I think of the pain of it all.

The pain of life.

For all our feigned gaiety, my court is not the same now. I can replace Anne with a new queen, I can replace my Boleyn courtiers with Seymours; I can substitute my original, trusted advisors with new, and my old friends with younger ones, but I cannot restore my own youth, my gaiety, or my optimism.

Anne has destroyed that; she has taken my joy with her. I will never again be the man I was before I knew her.

July - October 1536

The long-planned inspection of the defences at Dover cannot be postponed any longer and I decide to make a holiday of it. The royal party rides south, stopping at Rochester, Sittingbourne, and Canterbury on the way. I am not in the best spirits, but, as ever, I strive to conceal it from those around me. I summon a minstrel to ride close by and fill the drear hours of travel with song.

Of all the things that niggle at me, it is Jane's continuing monthly courses that disappoint me the most. I thought she would be pregnant by now; Lord forbid that I have taken another barren wife.

I try to force my mind away from the matter of sons and what will happen to England after my demise. I am determined to make the most of the season and on one hunt we kill twenty stags in a single day.

Plans for Jane's coronation are underway, but I hesitate to set a date until she fulfils her part of the bargain. It will be better if I can crown a queen whose belly is big with my child, the people will take it as an omen of good fortune to come. Coronations are always costly, but I am determined to put on as good a show as possible and order only the best of everything.

The best furnishings, the best clothing, the best jewels – Jane is my queen, my first indisputably *legitimate* queen, and I want the world to know it. It may be late in coming but I have almost all that I need now … all but one small thing.

As the summer waxes, my leg begins to pain me again and I struggle to maintain my habitual gaiety. Oh, I put on a show of merriment for the benefit of my court but … sometimes it is a trial. All the mummers and musicians in the world cannot blot out the constant throbbing of my leg, or the relentless nagging of my mind.

Jane's belly remains stubbornly empty despite my attempts to fill it. And as for matters of state, well … it has become a burden of late. If only I could take a break from it, but I cannot simply hand the reins to someone else for a while; there is no respite for kings, even for a short time. Even when I am at leisure, I am liable to be interrupted by ministers, envoys, and they rarely come to me with good news; it is all complaints, complaints … complaints.

The closure of the monasteries, for instance. Instead of it being viewed as a benefit to the country, the people are up in arms about it. They are unconcerned that the church has been robbing us for years with their extortionate rents, monies for this, monies for that. I see nothing holy in taking payment from the very person whose soul you are promising to pray for. And, as Cromwell has pointed out, it is not seemly for the monasteries to be richer than the king, especially since I am now the head of the church in England.

Before my changes began to be put in place, the monies levied from my people were all siphoned off to Rome – every single coin! I will have no more of it. The wealth will be better spent in my hands. I am astonished that the people do not like it.

It is not just the lowly folk who mumble against the religious changes; even some members of my court have slipped away to their homes, no doubt muttering about me. The traditionalists blame Cromwell and think his ideas are merely a ploy to insinuate the New Learning into our realm. If they imagine they will be forced to worship a certain way, then they are blind. Such simple men cannot think for themselves, they have been misled by Rome for so long that they see any other approach to worship as the work of the devil.

Well, let the devil take them, then.

I cease scribbling, throw down my pen, and exhale so violently that it makes the candle flame dance.

"What is it, Henry?"

She had been sitting so quietly I'd forgotten Jane was there, squinting over her embroidery in the ill light. She pokes her needle into the cloth, puts down her work and comes to me, stands behind me and rubs my shoulders. It should be reassuring, soothing to my mind, relaxing my body, but instead I find her ineffectual touch merely irritating.

Instead of relaxing back into her ministrations, I continue the internal tirade aloud. I let my hand fall on the pile of parchment still awaiting my attention.

"The constant complaints against the monastic closures are infuriating; the protests are hindering Cromwell's progress. Why can the people not see it is all for their benefit?"

She is silent for a moment, but she ceases her ministrations. When I turn to look at her, she straightens her shoulders and stands taller, clasping her hands so tightly her knuckles turn white.

"Your Majesty, the people have relied on the abbeys for years ... forever, in fact. The monks have offered employment, healing, and nurture in time of need. Even if you dismiss the spiritual side, the worship, and the guidance ... the monks offer aid for the practicalities of life. Where are the people supposed to turn once the monasteries are no more? It all seems shortsighted to me, rashly thought out. Rather than widespread dissolution, could the remaining foundations not be reformed instead, rather than closed ...?"

Dumbstruck, I stare at her white, rigid face, her terrified eyes. It is clear she already regrets speaking out. Perhaps she is possessed; mayhap the spirit of my last queen, who constantly proffered almost the very same argument, has taken hold of her.

I watch as her courage dwindles and she panics and scrabbles for my hand, tries to grasp it, but I withdraw it and coldly wave her away.

"Be quiet, woman, these matters do not concern you. You are not equipped to understand ..."

A peculiar look passes over her face, an expression I have not seen her assume before. It takes a moment before I recognise it as stubbornness. She looks like a mule.

"But I *do* understand, Henry. I understand perfectly well and greatly mislike what I am seeing happening to our loyal and pious monastic community. Should we, as monarchs, not nurture our subjects rather than condemn them to further poverty and suffering? The people need the ..."

"I said, BE QUIET!"

I stand up quickly, thrusting back my chair, and she scurries away from me, her hands to her mouth. I feel as if I have nourished a viper in my bosom.

"You, Madam, would do well to remember your place, and the fate of those who came before you. It is your job, nay your DUTY, to GIVE ME A SON, nothing more than that. Matters of politics do not concern you at all. Do you understand?"

She nods whitely, her mouth opening and closing, tears spilling down her flaccid cheeks. Damn the woman.

"Get out. I wish to be alone."

Needing no second reminder, she spins on her heel and flees from my presence. As her footsteps fade, I wonder what on earth has happened to the meek and pleasing girl I once courted.

Somers, who has witnessed the confrontation, lets out a long whistle.

"Naughty, naughty!" he says, retrieving a parchment that has floated to the floor and handing it to me. I take it and place it on the pile with the others.

"Naughty indeed, Will. She deserves a spanking."

Are all women deceivers? Does their entire sex pretend to be sweet and accommodating in order to lure men into marriage, to trick us with promises of fertility and obedience?

I fear it is so.

In the north of the country, where poverty is more predominant than piety, the people protest the loudest. There have already been riots about the shortages wrought by the harvest failure and discontent is rife but, in October, Cromwell brings word of more widespread trouble.

He stands before me, his features dour.

"It began after the closure of Louth Abbey, Your Majesty. The initial protest was modest; it was led by one of the monks, and a shoemaker ... of all people."

He pauses, as if expecting me to be amused at this.

"And?"

He fumbles with his papers.

"And their support rapidly grew and descended into a rabble, Your Majesty. One might call it outright rebellion. One of our officers, erm ... a Dr John Raynes, was dragged from his sickbed and beaten, Your Majesty, and his registers and accounting books were stolen and burned."

"Was he badly beaten?"

I frown at Cromwell, wondering what devil can have got into my subjects.

"Erm ... he was beaten to death, Your Majesty."

"To death? This isn't just a protest, it's rebellion, treason! The ring leaders will hang for this!"

"Yes, Your Majesty. I would not have disturbed you had the matter not been serious."

He draws forth a parchment, unrolls it and provides me with a summary of its content.

"Their demands are as follows. They require a halt to any further dissolution of religious houses, an end, or perhaps a further revision, to the Ten Articles. They require the collection of subsidies to cease, and no more peacetime taxes. They also demand a purge of your government. They make a point of mentioning 'baseborn councillors' which I assume means me, and they also insist that all 'heretics' should be removed from office. They require a repeal of the Statute of Uses, oh, and the protection of Lincolnshire church treasures and the right to continue to worship the Roman church in the old way."

"This is outrageous! May God damn them all to Hell."

"Yes, Your Majesty."

He closes his eyes, bows his head as if about to read a prayer.

"How many rebels are we talking of, Cromwell? How many ingrates are we dealing with?"

"An estimated forty thousand, Your Majesty."

"FORTY thousand?"

He flinches beneath my incredulity. "How can this be? Forty thousand subjects out in force against their king? How can we deal with this? Can we hang so many, Cromwell? Is it even possible?"

I snatch up a cup and frown into it, put it down again, slopping wine on the table. I had thought the common folk loved me, but it seems I was wrong.

"To be frank, Your Majesty, they claim no argument against you personally, and do not dispute your rule; their issue is just with this one small matter of policy."

I bring my cup down onto the table so hard that pain shoots up my arm. Rubbing my elbow, I scowl at him.

"It is one and the same thing, Cromwell, you know that."

"I do, Your Majesty," he replies wryly, "but it seems … they do not …perhaps understand."

"Send for Brandon. He must take his troops north to quell this outrage, and send for Norfolk, too. Their combined armies should be enough to send the rebels scurrying home. Men shall die for this, Cromwell, you have my word on that."

I wave him away, pour myself another cup of wine and stare into the fire.

In the weeks and months that follow, men do die but it doesn't halt or even hinder the protest. Just as the Lincolnshire rising is quelled, another demonstration springs up to take its place, this time in Yorkshire. Among other demands, they complain about the treatment I have given Kate and Mary. Well, I can't do anything about Kate now. She is dead, and Mary has been reinstated in my family and welcomed back to our court, if not the succession. Some of them even go as far as to decry the death of Anne – a woman they hated, a traitor to both the crown and state!

"It seems to me, Cromwell, that they are clutching at straws, and just digging up any small reason they can think of to throw at me."

"Ingrates, Your Majesty, be assured that they will receive just punishment when this is over."

"But how will we quell it? There are so many. We can hardly charge in and wage open warfare on half the country; and there are women and children involved."

"They are still rebels, Your Majesty, despite their age and gender. I suggest a show of force; it will likely scare them into submission. Perhaps Norfolk is the man to send but give him company, one of the large landowners with much to lose personally. They know Norfolk to be traditional in his method of religion; an ally in one regard at least. If that doesn't work and we cannot beat them by force of arms then I am afraid we will be forced to negotiate."

"Yes, you are right. Send Talbot too. Gah, but it goes against the grain to *negotiate* with traitors. Who are the leaders?"

He consults his papers.

"One Robert Aske, but I suspect he is a convenient figurehead concealing other, higher born men who secretly agree with the rebels' demands. Those are the voices who speak out against me in particular, Your Majesty, having a grudge against my low birth."

I look up, surprised that he should mention it.

"Your blood may be weak, man, but your wit is sharp, and that is all that matters in a statesman."

"I am gratified that you see it that way, Your Majesty."

Our eyes meet and I hesitate before speaking.

"I'd be lost without you, you know that."

His face opens in pleasure and flushes red as he stutters a mutual attachment. It is seldom he has no ready reply on his tongue.

While Jane makes ready for a merry Christmas celebration and prepares apartments fit to house my daughter, Mary, December is spoiled by the continuing events in the north. The rebels have now taken possession of York. Without forethought or consideration, they have reopened closed religious houses, turned out the new tenants and let the brotherhood back in.

My rage knows no bounds and I am allowed no outlet for it. I can feel it simmering beneath my skin. If I were a fit man, I would take up arms and ride against them myself. Since the situation is unprecedented, my council is at a loss as to what to do, and each meeting is loud, riotous, and ends in stalemate.

"We must calm the situation. Give them false promises. Once they have dispersed, they will be easier to deal with."

Cromwell makes it sound easy, but for once he is in error, and when Norfolk and Talbot meet with the rebel leaders and put our compromise on the table, they struggle to reach acceptable conclusions.

While hordes of 'pilgrims', as they are calling themselves, litter the roads around York, the rebels refuse to see reason. It takes all Cromwell's cunning to devise a plan that will perhaps persuade them to consider a truce.

At Pontefract castle, the leaders meet with us once more so a mutually acceptable document can be drawn up, listing their demands. There is a short respite while, fobbed off with promises of a general pardon for all, Aske dismisses the rebels, and the ragged 'pilgrims' disperse to their homes ... if they have them.

But my relief is shortlived, and when Cromwell next attends upon me, my peace of mind is broken once more.

"Are you convinced, Your Majesty, that Norfolk has actually achieved success?"

"Well, they have all gone home, haven't they? We have a peace, for now, at least."

"But, Your Majesty, think about it. Norfolk, with his vast army, his blustering power and influence, could only bring about peace by use of empty promises. I hope I am wrong, Your Majesty, but perhaps it would be unwise to forget Norfolk's love for the old faith. Is there a chance, do you think, that he dealt gently with the rebels because secretly he sympathised with their cause?"

"What are you saying? Do you think Norfolk is a traitor?"

He holds up both hands in protest.

"No, no, Your Majesty, not at all but ... one does wonder why he was so diligent in avoiding violence. He does not usually tread so softly. I have always understood he relished a fight."

"I think it had more to do with the vast number of rebels they faced, man. They were outnumbered. Forty thousand rebels to his five thousand and Talbot's seven thousand. In all the years I've known him, Norfolk has never flinched away from battle, but neither has he acted rashly."

"Although the rebels were largely unarmed."

I wave my arm to shut him up.

128

"Let it go, man. It would have been slaughter. The slaughter of my subjects. He may have given promises, but those boons were unendorsed by me. At a later date, when the crisis has lessened and the weather has improved, we can send more men, more arms, and take the rebels down by force if we have to. I would rather not, of course, for we must remember that they are simply misguided; they are not evil men. They have strayed a little from their shepherd, that is all."

"Hmm." Cromwell looks unconvinced but has the sense to pursue the subject no further. "And in the meantime, Aske is invited to court for Christmas?"

His raised left eyebrow slowly returns to its usual position when I beam at him.

"He is indeed, Cromwell, and once I have him in my presence, we shall see who is the better negotiator; my lord of Norfolk, or his king."

I sit on my throne, looking down from the dais upon the dancing and merriment. Jane is beside me; she is quiet and a little green about the gills, something that offers me hope. Mentally, I count back the weeks on my fingers and wonder if she might be with child. It is still too early to tell. I will wait a while before I question her, but I can't help allowing myself to dream. She has probably eaten some bad fish or caught a chill.

I turn slightly in my chair and examine her more closely. As I watch, she stirs herself, sits forward in her seat to applaud the antics of Will Somers, who is dancing with Mary's fool, co-incidentally named Jane.

They career around the hall in a gauche mockery of the queen and I; bumping into the other dancers, tripping over Cut and Ball and leaving chaos in their wake. It doesn't matter how much unrest there may be outside the bounds of court, within it, there is always jollity.

Amusement bubbles in my chest, and I reach for Jane's hand.

"You are almost as pretty as that other Queen Jane," I say, and she glances at me quickly, puzzlement on her brow, before looking away again. I follow her gaze about the milling hall.

Laden tables, dislodged greenery, dogs cleaning up dropped scraps from the floor, their tails waving. In the centre of the hall, the stately dance is growing wilder. I would love to join in, show them all that I am as lithe as I ever was, but I know better than to even attempt it. Every so often, the sores on my leg heal over, preventing the pus from escaping; at these times, the pain becomes unbearable, and the physicians are forced to open up the wound again. It is the only way I can be afforded some relief.

This evening, my leg is throbbing as it often does after a surfeit of food and wine, and the fastenings on my doublet are straining. I suppress a belch and watch a page creep up and grab a servant girl from behind. He kisses her soundly and her surprised screech drifts across to me. I sit up, alert lest her protest be in earnest, but relax again when she pulls from his arms and backs away, laughing and wiping her mouth on the back of her hand. As she slides behind a curtain, she calls something out to him, but her response is swallowed by the other sounds of merriment. From the expression on his face, her retort must have been astounding.

I would love to know what she said.

Another girl enters, a tray laden with drinks nestled on her hip, and the lad's attention switches to her. He watches her weave through the throng and, as if sensing his interest, she turns and smiles, gives him a bold wink.

I remember the days of my youth when I would go incognito with Brandon, George Boleyn, and Henry Norris to the inns across the river. There I would mix with my subjects, listen to them praise their brave, young King Hal. Had they known he was in their midst, I wonder if their behaviour would have remained as free and easy.

I was still a prince when I first took a Southwark wench on my knee; it's where I learned how to kiss, learned how a woman can tease and trick a man into letting go of his senses.

Those were dark, secret, magical days … days that will never come again. It is hard to go anywhere in disguise now, I am so big and noticeable, and my likeness hangs in every town hall. They would know me right away. I sigh deeply, regretful, mourning that bright, green boy and his companions, most of whom are now dead.

Beside me, Jane gasps, pulling me back from reminiscing on my murky past to the bright lights of the present.

"Master Aske is taking to the floor," she says, her voice high pitched with surprise. I narrow my eyes, squint through the torch light.

"He doesn't look very comfortable."

"No, and he is clearly very much out of practice, but he is smart in his new coat."

"It surprises me that a man so full of disdain for our policies and our way of life can find enjoyment in so trivial a pastime as dancing."

I watch the red velvet coat I gave him weave an uncertain way through the revellers. He hops, one beat behind the other dancers, as he attempts to learn the steps. Perhaps I should have thought to offer him an hour or two with the dance master, instead of endowing him with an expensive coat.

Jane notices my frown.

"Oh, Henry. Do not worry so. Once Christmas is over and Aske has travelled home to the north, he will spread the news of your indulgence, and things will be well again in the realm."

"Even though I have no intention of doing as they ask."

She looks down at her lap, her chin doubling, her mouth turning downward while she fiddles with her girdle.

"I wish you would listen to some of their demands at least, Henry."

I snatch my hand from her knee.

"Do not start. You had your way with Mary; I will have mine with the traitorous monks."

Seated at my left, Mary leans forward, speaks loudly above the din.

"Did you speak to me, Your Majesty? I thought I heard my name. I can barely hear above the music ..."

I lean toward her, our heads almost touching.

"I was just saying to the queen how splendid you look in your new gown. You should be dancing with the other young people."

She laughs, throws up her chin, reminding me of Kate.

"I would, Your Majesty, but nobody has dared to ask me."

I scan the hall, catch the eye of Jane's brother, Tom, and summon him to our table. He hurries forward, weaving through the throng, and makes a sweeping gallant bow before us.

"Your Majesty, how can I be of service?"

I beckon him closer so I might speak into his ear.

"Be so good as to dance with my daughter, would you, Tom?"

He bows again, smiles widely before backing away to make a leg before Mary who, with scarlet cheeks, allows him to take her hand and lead her to the floor.

"That was kind, Henry." Jane's eyes glisten with gratitude. I wave away her praise as if it is smoke from a candle.

"I would dance myself if I could. There is nothing I would like more than to take you onto the floor, but my leg is troublesome today."

As I ease my foot into a more comfortable position on the stool, her lower lip protrudes with sympathy.

"I am so sorry, Henry. When we retire, I will rub some of that salve that Lady Lisle sent you. You haven't tried it yet and she swears it soothes the most stubborn pain."

I grunt with displeasure. For all her effort to change the subject I have not overlooked her obvious, if unspoken, championing of the monks. She is not the only one with sympathies.

Rome, still interfering in the business of our realm, has installed my cousin as a new cardinal. Reginald Pole, long exiled from England for offences against the crown, now attempts to form a European offensive against me. He publishes pamphlets, flights of fancy that are full of lies and inconsistencies. It is all very well to be courageous while an ocean lies between us, and the Bishop of Rome is on his side, but if he were here before me now, in my realm, I know it would be a different matter.

I'd have his head.

I rest my chin on my fist and peer unseeing across the hall. That matter is not forgotten. Pole might be out of my reach, but his family are not. They are of Plantagenet descent; their mother, Margaret, being the daughter of George, my grandfather's uncle. They've always lusted for my crown. Margaret Pole has been under observation by Cromwell for some time but now, the entire family will be watched; the Courtneys too. I know they resent me and will slip up one day. Let them make just one wrong move against me or my heirs, and they will be swiftly dealt with.

Later, in the privacy of her chamber, with the music still sounding in my ears, I lie on Jane's bed. I wish now I had not indulged so freely at the feast, for my leg is agony and I have a pain beneath my ribs that often accompanies a surfeit of rich food.

Her hands are icy as she tentatively applies the salve to my leg. It stings a little at first, but soon I become used to it and the pain recedes a little. As the relief allows me to relax, I become more aware of the touch of her tiny cold fingertips and my mind turns to further intimacies.

"My thigh is aching too," I say, and after the slightest hesitation, she slowly works her way above my knee, small cold fingers reaching higher … and higher. I hold my breath, longing for her to take the initiative, to take me in hand as Anne would have done, but instead she stops and sits uncertainly back on her heels.

With a groan of frustration, I thump the mattress.

"Jane! I am your husband!"

She crinkles her brow and bites her lip as if it is our first time. With a roar of displeasure, I pull her down upon the pillows and push aside her voluminous bed gown, while she lies beneath me; passive, compliant, and wholly unexciting.

<u>April - August 1537</u>

The first few months of the year are always tediously long, but this year they seem interminable and bleaker than ever. I am glad when April arrives. The people of the north revolt yet again and although the rebels are fewer this time, my patience has come to an end and so has my leniency.

Once more, I send Norfolk and Suffolk in haste to deal with it and this time their orders are to show no mercy.

The people used to love me. Whenever I travelled about the country, I was greeted with cries of joy, cheers of pride, but now there are grumbles around every shadowy corner, and every one of my decisions is questioned.

They must learn that I am the king, and my decisions are final. As God's representative, I cannot be in error, but with their faith in me waning, I need a son and England needs a prince to bolster our security. A boy will guarantee the continuance of Tudor rule.

No matter how I try, I can find no peace, not even in prayer. My leg aching, I stumble from the chapel, uncomforted by the commune with God as I was in my younger days. It is as though He has turned from me, and I am at a loss as to what I must do to please Him. Until I learn what He requires of me, I will continue to be denied everything I have ever desired.

All winter I have watched my queen, and even now the spring is here I still wait for her to show signs of the long-promised pregnancy. My hopes were raised at Christmastide but … they came to nothing.

I spend every possible night I can in her bed, loving her for as long and as often as my body allows. Nobody could accuse me of not doing my duty. I am a martyr to it; it is Jane who is not doing hers.

The fear that I have married another barren woman continues to grow; am I cursed? Is this God's punishment for some long-forgotten sin?

When I think of the meanest hovels in my realm that are teeming with undernourished, unwanted boys, I could weep! The lowliest folk in the land are blessed, while I, their pious, faithful, and loving king am denied one living son.

But then, in early April, I arrive unannounced at Jane's apartments and find her drooping over a bowl. She looks up, green-faced, with traces of vomit on her chin and joy stabs me, just below the heart.

She wipes her mouth on her sleeve.

"Oh Henry, my husband," she wails through damp stringy hair. "I believe I may be with child at last."

As she crawls toward me, delight swims up from my belly and floods my being.

"So I see!"

Forgetting my injuries, I grab both her hands and drag her around the chamber in a wild jig. Will Somers whirls around with us, delight on his wide face. Jane limps after me, her face pale, her head lolling and, belatedly, I consider her condition. I stop abruptly and Will cannons into us, falling to the floor. The spaniels, thinking it a game, try to lick his face.

"Apologies," I say and beckon a woman to bring a chair. I ease Jane into it. "I noticed you've been downcast of late," I say. "I thought it was on account of those accursed monks. When do you expect my son to arrive?"

She accepts a cup from her woman and drinks deeply, then dabs at her lips with a kerchief.

"I cannot say for certain, but I think perhaps, in the autumn ... I am unschooled in such matters."

"September then, or October perhaps. Plenty of time to arrange things. I will order the nursery to be made ready. You will have fun choosing the fabrics and trimmings; Mary can help you. We must find a wet nurse. I will summon Lady

Bryan; she will know of one. She had the care of Elizabeth and …"

I stop suddenly, remembering belatedly that I have been in this position many times before. This is not the first time a queen has promised me a prince and then reneged by bringing forth a girl … a useless girl, or even worse, a dead boy.

I frown, and suddenly morose, I wave a hand at Jane.

"See to it that you attend to your diet. I read somewhere that certain foods ensure the gestation of a male child. I will search out the book and instruct the physicians to advise you. I will leave you now. See that you rest, do not strain yourself. Stay in bed … for the whole term if you must."

I return to my own apartment, sit at my desk and begin to compile a list, but the brief surge of joyful longing in my heart has already been replaced by fear, and by dread.

My fingers drum agitatedly on the desk. She must give me a son, she *must*, or it will all have been for nothing. My entire adult life will have been wasted.

"Ah, Your Majesty. I must offer you my congratulations …" Norfolk enters, sweeps off his cap and bows low.

"Norfolk," I grunt, beckoning him forward, and he approaches as if on broken limbs. "What is it, man? Why do you limp?"

"Oh," his thin lips curl upward. "Just my usual complaint, Your Majesty. The physicians say it is merely the damp seeping into my ageing bones."

He is well past his prime. Mentally, I count backward, trying to gauge his age.

"What age are you now, I can't recall a time when you weren't at court …"

"I am not certain, but I believe I have passed my sixtieth year, Your Majesty."

"Good grief, man, you are in your dotage. Pull up a stool. You may sit in my presence. It is time you retired permanently to your estates, is it not? Although what in Heaven I'd do without you, I don't know."

He laughs, a lifetime of campaigning in the gritty sound. "Never, Your Majesty, not as long as I can mount my horse and serve my country ... and my king."

He bows his head and winces as he accepts my offer of a seat. I cough to disguise how touched I am by his devotion and summon a boy to fill our cups. One of the dogs is scratching at the chamber door to come in.

"So, what news of the rebels?"

"As you know, the north is now quiet ... the discontent continues and there is simmering resentment against the hangings – we took a few from each settlement, around seventy in all – but ... well, if men insist on rebelling it is what they must expect."

"Exactly. I do not know what gets into these northerners. Even in my grandfather's day there was trouble up there."

"... and even previous to that, Your Majesty."

"Precisely, Norfolk. Perhaps it's something to do with the cold."

"In that case, you think they'd remain by their firesides!"

He gives a raucous guffaw, and we clash our cups together, silence following while we sup our wine. The dog is yelping now. I signal to a page to let him in, and the next few minutes are spent trying to dissuade Cut from licking my face.

"And the leaders?" I ask, wiping drool from my cheek. "They have been brought south for trial?"

I clamp the dog between my knees, squeeze him until he complies and sits quietly. Norfolk continues the conversation as if nothing is happening.

"Yes, Your Majesty, we've arrested Aske, Darcy, and Thomas Constable and some others whose names escape me. They will remain in the Tower for a time, to consider their actions ... before the hearing. Cromwell has all that in hand."

He cannot speak Cromwell's name without sneering, and the rivalry between the highborn peer and the lowly tradesman's son amuses me. I laugh, but then, as his words sink in, I pause.

"But justice must be seen to be done, Norfolk. The trial must be fair."

"Of course," he says, "and now I suppose, if there is nothing else you wish to discuss, I must take some time to call upon my daughter. She will be as full of complaint as always."

I do not reply. The less we discuss her, the better. Mary Howard continues to make a fuss about failing to receive a widow's pension from Fitzroi's estate, but since their union was not consummated, it was no true marriage and therefore she was no true wife. The pension can remain where it is, in my coffers. There is plenty of time for her to remarry.

Norfolk, noting my silence, takes it as a signal to leave and struggles to his feet, makes a bow. I keep hold of Cut, watch Norfolk move across the room and, just before he disappears from view, I remember something.

"Norfolk!"

He turns, lifts his head, and waits for me to speak. "That fellow Aske, see that he hangs. His failure to keep his promise to maintain the peace cannot go unpunished."

"Of course, Your Majesty." He bows again and takes his leave.

I hardly dare let myself hope as Jane's belly swells and she seems to be thriving. Perhaps, for once, God is on my side. Perhaps, my long wait for an heir will soon be at an end.

An image rises in my mind of a fair-haired child, a boy with a bold smile and a ready wit – a boy full of vitality and mischief. But I push the pleasing image away and try not to think of it. It does not do to hope. I have done so too many times.

Fear stays with me. The certainty that I will again be disappointed battles with my desire for things to go well. My fear ensures that I visit Jane's apartments almost daily. I keep regular checks on her health and enquire every morning that she has all she needs. Quails seem to figure highly on her list of requirements and a regular supply is sent in by Lady Lisle. The queen cannot seem to get enough of this particular dish, and I tease her, declaring she would break her fast on them if her morning sickness allowed.

Concerned that her sickness is lasting well beyond the fifth month, I consult the physician, but he assures me it is just the way with some women.

"And that is not a sign of anything lacking. It will not prevent her from bearing me a healthy son?"

He laces his fingers together.

"There is no reason why she should not, Your Majesty. The queen is slightly old to be carrying her first child, but she is healthy and strong. I fully expect a happy outcome."

Relief floods through me. As long as the child thrives, Jane can put up with the minor inconvenience of a little early morning puking. Better women than she have done so.

Processing along the corridor in search of her, I pause to speak to a courtier who was recently suffering from a sore and flaking scalp.

"Ah," I say, examining his head while he makes his bow, "was the lotion I provided for your rash effective? I have not yet used that one and would welcome your opinion on it."

"I've been meaning to thank Your Majesty," he replies once he is upright again. "The lotion was most effective; the itching stopped almost instantly, and the rash cleared up rapidly after that, once I'd stopped scratching it."

"Excellent, my grandmother always scolded us if we scratched. 'You are not puppies,' she used to say."

I laugh aloud at the memory, and he laughs with me, before bowing low again as I move on, leaving him gratified, his day made perfect by the attention of his king.

I am in good spirits; for once my leg is not paining me over much, and there is a new song on my lips. Only the last few lyrics are escaping me, but I know I will have it perfected by the end of the afternoon. I will try it out on the queen after dinner. Anne was always a great help when I was struggling with a new tune. I see no reason why Jane should not be also.

The doors to the queen's apartments are thrown open at my approach, the ladies scuttle to the far reaches of the room, fall to their knees in homage. By the open window, my queen waits for me, the sunshine gilding her hair. She looks up, wipes tears from her face and hastily pulls on her coif. I halt, look about the room, searching for the source of her sorrow.

"What is it? What has made you weep? What has happened?" I stare accusingly at her women, none of whom meets my eye.

"Well?" I almost shout. "What is the matter? Is it the child? Shall I call a physician?"

"No, no, Henry. I am quite well. It is … something else."

I wave her women away and obediently they quit the chamber, the door closes, leaving us alone.

"What is it, Sweetheart?" I ask more gently. "Come, sit with me."

Submissively, she gets up and joins me on the window seat, and I pull her onto my knee, my hands trailing down to cradle her belly. The contact sends a little shrim of pleasure through me. It always does me good to feel the solidity of the living child within.

"What is it?" I ask for the third time. "Have you run out of quails?"

She gives a watery laugh and settles deeper into my lap, a hand sliding about my neck.

"Oh, Henry, sometimes I feel so very afraid."

I squeeze gently.

"There is no need for that. I am here to protect you. I will always keep you safe."

Unbidden, Anne's face rises in my mind's eye, but I push her away, back to her tomb. She was never afraid of anything, and if she was, she never let on.

"Come, tell me, Jane; you are my beloved queen. I will do all in my power to make you happy."

She pauses, sits up and wipes her face. It is blotched and pale, her eyes red and her nose is beginning to run. My belly squirms in distaste. I look away.

"I worry, Henry, after what happened in York …"

My heart sinks. She means Aske. Someone has told her he is still hanging in chains from the walls of the castle, and

140

she is worried that God will punish us for inflicting such a slow agonising death. She doesn't understand that Aske is the sinner, and I am guided by God. To speak against me, as God's representative, is to speak against God Himself. Aske chose his fate, not I.

I cover her hand with mine.

"Jane," I say gently, as if addressing a child. "God speaks through me. It is His will."

"Really?" She does not look convinced.

"Of course. All sinners must be punished. It is an unpleasant duty, but it is my task to see that His will is done."

She looks down at her belly, my jewelled fingers caressing it.

"What about Mary?"

She speaks into her chest. I see her bite her lip, close her eyes as if sending up a swift prayer that I will harken to her request this time.

"Mary? What about her?"

She shifts on my knee, looks up at me with hope and enthusiasm writ large upon her face. At least she isn't weeping for once.

"I would so like to see her happy. She needs a husband, she needs children – they would be your grandchildren, Henry! Think of that! Dom Luis is a great match ..."

"Hmm."

I do think of it. Often. I think of Mary's future children – strong boys growing up, realising who their grandfather is and challenging my own son for the crown. I think of the possible conflict, the treason and war that might follow. I think of insurrection. The Tudors thwarted, a foreigner on the throne of England: Tudor blood diluted - half Spanish, half Portuguese.

It would never do.

Blithely, I decide to prevaricate, and pat her hand. "I will think on it. I would have Cromwell's opinion on the matter before I make my final decision on so important a subject."

My promise to consider the match gains me some respite from her demands. If I dissemble long enough, the child will be born, and I can then refuse the proposed marriage between Mary and Dom Luis without fear of upsetting the queen and causing her to miscarry.

Mary is, however, a continuing problem, yet I am glad of the reconciliation between us. I loved her dearly when she was an infant. She was always a good girl until the trouble began between me and the qu- ... and Kate. Yet that pretty little girl has matured into a plain woman whose disgruntlement with life is written large on her face.

Mary has become the sort of woman for whom husbands are difficult to find. Without the lure of a royal title, we should perhaps be glad that anyone is willing to take her, but still ... her marriage will always pose a risk.

I find joy in the flourishing relationship between Mary and the queen; the girl is a welcome addition to our court. Mary plays a good game of chess; she is not a skilled musician but is musical nonetheless, with a keen ear and good taste. Her chambers are always full of melody and merriment. I like to think she inherited that from me and not her dour mother, although, thinking on it, Kate was fond of music too and not always glum.

In our youth, Kate shone as brightly as a star. I can still recall the way my heart lifted whenever she entered a room. The way my palms grew moist, and my words became difficult when she directly addressed me. Although I'd never have admitted it then, I was a green boy ... and she was kind when few other people were.

"Henry?" Kate's young face is replaced by Jane's pale, puffed features and I realise I have been daydreaming. I give myself a shake.

"You were saying?"

She laughs. "I was saying that perhaps we should ask Mary to join us for supper one evening. Just a private supper, the three of us, before it is time for me to enter confinement."

"Yes, if you wish. I will be leaving Hampton Court soon. The plague grows worse, and I should move the court to safer ground."

"Oh," she frowns. "I thought – I understood my confinement was to take place here. Was I misinformed?"

I pat her hand and she grips my fingers tightly.

"No, you are quite right. It will be here. The arrangements have been made. You shall stay. The contagion will hardly find its way into the lying-in chamber. It would never dare venture past your fierce women."

"N-no."

She laughs nervously and looks down again at our clasped hands. Despairing at her lack of humour, I wriggle my fingers free and ease her to her feet.

"I must go. Cromwell is waiting on me this afternoon. I will call on you again soon. Make sure you rest and eat properly. You need your strength."

She watches me go, her eyes full of fear, her chin trembling with repressed tears. Only the Lord knows what ails her now, so I pretend not to notice. I hope God forgives my little lie about meeting with Cromwell. My leg being almost free of pain today, I am determined to burn off a surfeit of energy before the day is over. My horse is already saddled and has been waiting so long he will be growing restless. It is not too late in the day to ride out; I may even have my hawk brought out of the mews for an airing.

I should have listened to the advice of the physicians for, within days of my hunting trip, the ulcer on my leg breaks out again. My spirits plummet. The pain is immense; it is all I can do not to strike out at those closest to me.

I try to carry on as usual but during the morning Mass I grind my teeth, speaking through clamped jaws. I send for the physicians, but all the salves and poultices they can muster do not even begin to ease it.

It is too hard to concentrate, I cannot focus on matters of state but, somehow, I drag myself to the meeting. The session is interminable; I snap at my council, I thump

Cromwell on the side of his head, and scowl at the amusement this evokes among the other men – his enemies.

It wasn't supposed to be like this. *I* wasn't supposed to be like this. I intended to be a kindly king, a king beloved of the people, a wise, learned, and benevolent king, and I hate myself for being the opposite. To my great shame, I am living up to the name that some whisper against me. The name they think I know nothing of. *Old Mouldwarp* or, if they are feeling more kindly, King Herod.

Yet once I have done my duty and Jane has given me an heir, they will learn to love me again. A boy is on the way. The country is stable and the Church of Rome, which was once extorting us, is now repelled. We are at last free to move forward and worship God without the intervention of foreigners. My good servant, Cromwell, and I have made it so. Things will get better now. I can concentrate on building ships, improving our navy, constructing castles and forts along our shores to secure us against foreign attack.

Yet until I have that son, my achievements will continue to be ignored. I must ensure the Tudor regime is celebrated, as saviours, something to mark my triumphs that will last long into the future, something that men will speak of long after I am dead.

I lie awake at night, racking my brains to think of a way, but it is almost morning when I finally come up with an idea. I smile widely into the lightening dawn and thump my pillow with satisfaction. I will send for Holbein in the morning.

The artist has been at court frequently of late, making sketches of the queen and her ladies in readiness for Jane's coronation likeness to be made. But while he is here, I shall commission him to paint another canvas, and this one will be a huge mural for the privy chamber at Whitehall Palace. A mural to celebrate not just me and my heirs, but the roots from which we sprang.

My leg is troublesome again, ulcers that I had thought healed have broken open once more; the pus that oozes from the sores is almost as noxious as the stench of the salve they daub upon it. The only thing that distracts me from the pain is the planning of the painting, and when I grow bored with that, I turn my thoughts to other things. I plan improvements to the many properties I have recently acquired; monastic properties that cry out to be extended and converted into magnificent homes. I will refurbish the buildings and install vast gardens, with fountains and pleasances the like of which England has never seen.

Before the summer has reached its peak, the plague is rife in London, sometimes taking upwards of a hundred victims a day. Fearful for my unborn son, I forbid anyone from the city entry to the court. Jane is as terrified of infection as I, and so she should be. The pestilence takes high and low-born folk alike so, while Jane and her women keep to the safety of her apartments, I make only short hunting forays, careful to remain within a day's ride of the palace.

But, as the heat increases, so does the contagion, and men's lusts rise along with it. Tempers always run high in the summer and this year is no exception. The Earl of Surrey, a man I have ever found amusing and irritating in turns, develops a strange attachment to a daughter of the late Earl of Kildare.

The court is rife with whispers of the poetry he composes for her, the sonnets he pens in the depths of night. Lust is nothing new at court, of course it isn't, but the thing that makes this attachment so extraordinary is the fact that the object of his affection is but ten years old. That being so, I am confident no impropriety has taken place, but the court, men and women alike, are highly amused; teasing him to his face and laughing about him behind his back. The mockery seems to make no difference to Surrey.

I choose to ignore the matter until a fray breaks out between the Earl and Lord Beauchamp, and the resulting duel takes place within the Verge of the Court. I cannot overlook it any longer and action must be taken but, reluctant to make more of it than the matter deserves, I order him to a two-week confinement.

The court soon forgets, and Surrey spends his punishment writing verse dedicated to his Fair Geraldine. I imagine the girl in question is relieved to be spared his attentions and while Surrey is detained, the courtiers look around for another scandal.

The weather grows hotter, and everyone is tetchy. Even my sweet-mannered Jane becomes picky about her women's attire. Jane has never favoured the French style of hood that Anne and my sister, Mary, made so popular. She prefers a gabled hood, like Kate used to wear, but where previously she was lenient, she now becomes intolerant of anything in the French style and enforces new and rather stringent rules.

For the first time, there are murmurs of resentment toward her. When a new member of the queen's household arrives, something in her manner seems to rouse the queen's ire. She is a pretty child, born to Lady Lisle during her first marriage. When she is presented to the queen, my gentle Jane, usually so full of welcome to new girls, expresses her displeasure and orders her to be rid of her French hoods and adopt the gabled style; she also insists the girl avail herself of a velvet frontlet … without delay.

This is very much out of character, but when I quiz her on it later, Jane sniffs disdainfully and straightens her shoulders.

"I simply find the caps unattractive, Henry. I always have. I much prefer the gable style of bonnet. I have to look at my women all day, and I dislike them wearing that particular type, they remind me of …"

They remind her of Anne who championed everything French, but I do not prompt her to finish her sentence.

"It is not like you to impose such strictures on your women, though. Is there something about young Anne you mislike? There is no need for you to accept her into your household if you don't want to. Are you afraid her mother will cease to send your supply of quails?"

I laugh aloud at my joke, for Anne is the daughter of Lady Lisle, who has recently kept Jane so well supplied with her favourite treat, but Jane's responding smile is closer to a sneer.

Drumming my fingers on my knee, I look vaguely about the room to where her women are working at their embroidery. The only sound to break the silence is that of the lute player in the corner, and the sound of a small dog yapping outside to be admitted. My heart sinks. The dull claustrophobia of the chambers suddenly reminds me of Kate's. In the dying days of our marri- ... our relationship, I would visit her from time to time, where, suffocated by boredom, I longed only to escape to the vibrancy of Anne's apartments. I can't do that now.

But Jane will enter confinement in a few days; of course, it is natural for her to be tetchy and dull. Once the boy is born, we will celebrate in full measure and she will be her old self, her chambers will be gay ... as gay as a May Day parade.

I release her hand and stand up to take my leave and, as I pass between the bowing women, one of them glances up. She is young, and beneath the shadow of her ugly hood her eyes are dark and wide, dancing with mischief. For a moment, I forget to breathe. I pause; slightly bow my head in acknowledgement before I go on my way.

Doors open and close again behind us.

"Who is that lady?" I ask my attendant as I hobble back along the corridor that leads to my chambers. "The one with the dark eyes."

He offers me his arm and I take it, grateful for the support.

"That was Lady Anne Basset, I believe, Your Majesty. A newcomer to the queen's household."

Ah, I think, the one whose pretty French hood the queen took such exception to. The mystery is now solved. She has nothing against the woman's hood; it is her face she resents.

The queen is tearful as she makes ready to enter confinement. When I ask the reason for it, her face crumples and she lists a string of grievances. Her usual calm is transformed into near hysteria.

"I have spent the *whole* summer closeted away for fear of the plague. I long for fresh air yet I am now to be forced to endure a further month or more incarcerated in my chambers!"

It is not like Jane to complain. I place my knuckle beneath her chin and compel her to look at me. She blinks rapidly, a tear falls onto her cheek. She looks tired, jaded, and there are definite bags beneath her eyes.

I glance around at the closed shutters, the cloying soft furnishings, the drapes, and the leaping flames in the fireplace. It is over-warm and stuffy in here. I wouldn't wish to spend more than an hour in such a place, yet all has been prepared to keep the queen calm, to ensure that no harsh sounds, or images, or chill draughts affect the child. Even the tapestries are feminine; the woven scenes depicting tranquil meadows, fields of flowers and fountains, unicorns and rabbits.

"Come, come, Sweetheart. It is not so bad. It isn't a tomb. Look at the fine furnishings, the furs, the cushions, the best tapestries money can buy. Look at the ladies who are to be your companions. You do not hear them complain. They are joyful to be here because they are with you."

She pulls away, swallows, clenches her jaw and nods, but I recognise the mulish set to her chin. It is an expression I am beginning to see more often on my placid wife's face.

"I am sorry, Your Majesty. Forgive me for my ingratitude. I know it is my duty and I mean to make you proud."

"I will be proud when you present me with a son."

I pat her knee, ignoring the terror in her eyes, then I kiss her on the lips and, turning to her women, I address them directly.

"You must do everything in your power to amuse the queen. She is not to be allowed to fall into despondency. She must be entertained, cherished … nurtured. It is imperative that nothing impacts upon the child she is carrying, for he will be the future King of England."

As I near the end of the sentence, I raise my voice, turn it into a declaration, and a murmur of agreement runs around the chamber, a ripple of applause. I slide an arm about Jane's shoulders.

"There, you see? All will be well. All is in order. Now, I must go. I am riding out with Suffolk today, but I will be lodging at Esher, not too far away, and we will be reunited just as soon as the child is born."

She watches me leave. At the door, I turn for one last look. She is pale and sad, her mouth downturned, a green tinge to her skin, her belly as wide as a church door, her swollen ankles propped on a low stool. I wish she'd make more effort to appear merry; it does me no good to look upon such a glum face. Adopting a hearty smile, I blow her a kiss of encouragement, but she doesn't reach out to catch it.

9th – 12th October 1537

"It will be a boy, won't it, Brandon? I can't imagine God would be so cruel as to disappoint me again."

As the rest of the party falls back, Suffolk draws his horse closer to mine. He holds the reins in one hand, his hat at a jaunty angle, his smile wide and encouraging. Like me, his youth has passed, but he is still handsome with a goodly carriage and a magnetic charm.

"I pray daily for a prince, Your Majesty. The entire realm is begging God to make it so. I can envisage no other outcome."

I ease my horse to a halt and sit staring across the heath, where low-growing shrubs are dotted among the purple heather. In a nearby copse, the few remaining leaves cling to the branches like orange and red coins, resistant to the increasing winds.

The days are growing shorter now that autumn is here, and hints of the winter to come eddy about our knees. We must make as much of the clement weather as we can before the cold sets in hard. Before we know it, Christmas will be upon us, Jane will be back at court, and a new prince will sleep in the cot in the royal nursery. Tudor England will be saved.

"Jane was afraid when I took my leave of her last month. I wonder if the passing weeks have eased her fears or increased them."

"Afraid? Of the birth, you mean?"

"Aye, the birth. It's always hazardous, and then there is the chance of her being delivered of a girl. I confess I fear that more than anything."

He lets out a long breath and eases his hips forward in the saddle as he squints into the distance while carefully negotiating my question. At length, he turns his head to face me.

"If it should be a girl, and that girl is healthy, there is every chance the next child will be a boy. If it comes to the worst, Hal, you must cling to that."

Only Brandon would dare suggest such a thing. Everyone else assures me that God will surely smile on us, and that they are positive that, this time, my queen will bring forth a boy. I am glad he didn't try to humour me. I appreciate his honesty, his bravery … even though I abhor the insinuation behind his words. The strong possibility of a daughter – oh, God in Heaven, forbid!

"There is no *time*, Brandon. My youth has passed, I can feel age creeping into my bones, and there is grey in my beard. I need a son, and I need him now! I have required a son for a very long time. It seems so unfair …"

"All we can do is pray."

He hands me a flask and I take a slurp of wine that runs warm and thick to my belly.

"If she proves to be barren and loses the child I cannot divorce another wife nor take the head of another queen."

At least this one isn't crowned though; it would be easier.

It is as if a devil has come to sit on my shoulder to whisper evil into my ear. I push the unspoken thought away and silence tolls between us, the former merriment of the chase forgotten.

For me, at least.

It is all very well for Brandon, who now has two infant sons to replace those he lost, and his young wife has proven herself to be fertile enough to give him more. In fact, now I think of it, he is a grandfather too, for the daughter from his union with my sister, Mary, has recently given birth to a girl. I'm told they've named her Jane, after the queen. Thank God she is a girl and can pose no threat to my heirs. I glance at him, catching him staring bleakly into the distance.

"There will be no need for that, of course," I add, with feigned optimism. "Jane has never disappointed me yet. I can't see her beginning to do so now."

I gather up my reins and turn to shout over my shoulder.

"I'll race you back to the old oak!"

We ride like mad things across the moor. I'm just ahead, leaving the straggling courtiers far behind, but Brandon is close behind me. As I thunder through the dying light and the lengthening shadows of the heath, I acknowledge that, in truth, I am running from my own thoughts, the dread of what might soon come to pass.

Grateful that I can blame the tears on my cheeks upon the cold air and the speed with which I travel, I ride blindly toward the palace. In truth, though none must ever guess, I am broken by the lack of a male heir; my pride and my heart have been sore about the lack of a son for so long I can imagine nothing else. But if I am right and God sends me another useless daughter, it can only be a sign of His displeasure. I have no clue how I will deal with it.

The lights of Esher glow welcomingly in the evening gloom as Brandon canters after me into the palace yard. I slide from the saddle, toss the reins to a waiting groom, and the spaniels tumble, barking, from the hall to greet me. As I place my foot on the lower step to the hall, a messenger appears, with Norfolk at his elbow. Then I notice Cromwell grinning just behind. I draw off my gauntlet, let it fall. Someone scrambles to retrieve it.

"What is it?"

"He's coming, Sire. He will soon be here." I frown at Somers, who weaves and cavorts through the gathering crowd. Norfolk pushes him rudely aside.

"The queen, Your Majesty. Her pains have begun and, before the night is out, the child will be born."

What have they to grin about? I wonder. Now is not the time to be merry. Now, the day I have been dreading and longing for in turn has arrived. It is the time to pray, to hope, to make a deal with the devil if necessary.

I shove my hat at Cromwell and hurry up the steps. Skirting the hall that is teeming with waiting well-wishers, I look neither right nor left as I head for my private chapel.

Still clad in mud-spattered hunting clothes and ignoring the searing pain in my leg, I spend hours on my knees before the altar. The frigid cold bites into my bones, my hips and ankles cramping, my fingers fused. With cold sweat upon my brow, I lean my head on my clasped hands.

"Please, just send me a son, please send me a son, please send me a son …"

Over and over, I repeat it, as if my life depends on just one more repetition. As if there is a chance that my prayers will not only be heard, but answered too.

"I will do anything, give up anything, do anything, but please, dear God, just send me a son."

It is dawn when they finally pluck up the courage to lure me away from the altar to take some nourishment, to wash and change my soiled clothes, to slide between newly laundered sheets and try to sleep. I go through the motions as if I am under some enchantment, but the words of my prayer do not cease for a moment. They continue in my head in an endless reel, like a monkish chant. *I will do anything, but please just send me a son.*

The physicians were wrong when they said the boy would be born before nightfall. For three days, I wait and pray while the queen labours. Hourly, I send messengers to enquire if there is any news, but it is always the same.

The queen is struggling. It is not an easy birth and there are some difficulties in bringing the child forth. The voices in my mind argue, laying wagers on what will be.

It will be a boy, born dead or malformed. *By Christ, am I cursed?*

But the queen is strong and determined, and has not lost heart. He *must* be born alive.

He *must* be healthy. He must be a boy!

With tension screaming in my head, I increase my prayers, intoning the prayer aloud in an effort to drive out those devils' voices. I order that the court should pray with me. Everyone must pray; I order that the entire realm should do the same.

On the third day, a weary messenger limps into the chapel, his eyes red-rimmed, his clothes dishevelled, his face as pale as lead. I stare at him as if he is something horrid on my shoe, certain that he has come to tell me that my son has perished, that my hopes are dashed.

I brace myself, remind myself that, as king, I must at all costs hide the depths of my brokenness from the court. As he opens his mouth to speak, Norfolk elbows the messenger out of the way.

"Your Majesty! The queen has been delivered of a son!"

My heart turns a somersault. Sick hope swirls in my belly. I stare at him in astonishment. Can this be true? I suspect a trick, a mistake … and my voice, when it comes, is a mere whisper.

"A son? A living son?"

A great cheer echoes through the palace and I see that half the court has followed Norfolk into my presence. The chapel is bursting. Jane's brothers crowd forward, shaking people's hands, nodding their tousled heads, their worry replaced by euphoria.

We all know what it means to be the uncle of a future king. As my world erupts into joyful madness, Brandon pushes forward and, with great temerity, embraces me in a great bear hug. Our eyes lock.

"A son! Brandon, I have a son!"

I see the tears on his cheeks and weep into his fur collar while he thumps me on the back, his words of congratulation choked by happiness.

"I will go to her, at once. I must see him."

"But, Your Majesty, it is full dark. You must wait until morning."

"Must? There is no 'must' where I am concerned, Brandon. I will leave right away, and you may accompany me. It is not so far to Hampton Court; order up the torches and a guard. There is no time to be lost."

The corridor to the queen's apartment at Hampton Court seems unusually long. I hurry slowly, passing faceless courtiers, the hue of their gowns and cloaks merging, blurring into a rainbow at the corner of my eye.

I feel I am in a dream where the road I am travelling grows longer as the desire to reach my destination increases. Every step takes me farther away, each door that is thrown open at my approach reveals yet another threshold between me and my son, another obstacle. But at last, I am there.

Women, featureless women, fall to their knees when I enter. The room is still in some disarray, linen and unguents scattered on tables, draped across the floor. The bed is huge, it seems to sway like a landed ship in the centre of the chamber, the curtains around it like full-bellied sails. My eyes swivel away from the small woman in the centre of it and fasten on the royal cradle, which gently rocks a short distance away.

I am almost too afraid to approach. If I peek over the edge and look at the child, I may find it is only another dream. I may find a girl, or worse than that, a tiny corpse in a winding sheet. I hold my breath, take a step closer and suddenly remember another birth, in another chamber, in another reign.

I recall my mother, pale upon the bed, while I was shown another newborn sibling. Elizabeth, they named her, after the queen – a child who lasted just a few days longer than my mother did. The grief of losing her has never left me. I can still recall the scent of the chamber, the warmth of the roaring fire, the last gentle touch of her hand. With each passing year I miss her more, and the loss is impounded each and every time I am forced to bear the death of another child.

If I have learned one thing it is that children die, and sometimes mothers die, but *this* child - the boy in this cradle - this child must survive.

He must be strong.

At last, I am close enough to see him. He is awake, swaddled tight, his red face squashed and disgruntled, his nose bruised. As my lips stretch wide in delight, he scowls back at me, a bubble of spittle at the side of his mouth.

My heart swells.

I snap my fingers and the nurse comes running.

"Unbind him. I would look upon my son."

My son, those words I have waited so long to speak, fall so naturally from my lips. She scurries forward, lifts the child, who squawks loudly at the interference, his complaints growing in volume as the warm bands are loosened and the chill air of the chamber strikes his skin.

She lays him naked on the sheet and he throws out his limbs, scrawny, red limbs, like those of a skinned rabbit. His fists are clenched, his round belly heaving in rage, the scar of his navel bulging alarmingly. Between his thrashing legs I glimpse confirmation that he is indeed a boy; my son, my heir.

With immense joy, I scoop him up, cradle him against my chest until he quiets a little and begins to suck ferociously at his fist. I turn to the bed, where my green-faced wife is smiling.

"He is strong," I say, "and well-grown already. Look how hard he kicks."

At her signal, the queen's women help her rise higher on the pillow. She tucks the blankets beneath her arms and smoothes her hair.

155

"You have no need to tell me how hard he can kick, Henry, my bruised ribs have stood testament to that these past months."

Her voice is faint, pale almost. I laugh, lighter than I have felt for weeks, years. At last, God has shown me his favour and I have all I desire. My queen is fertile, my son is strong, my dynasty is at last secure, and we have so much time ahead in which to beget other sons and strengthen England even further.

With the Tudor line established, the people will be secure; they will have no need for rebellion. With one wave of his tiny infantile fist, this boy has dispelled dissention.

I draw my coat over his nakedness and turn to the queen.

"You have done well, Jane. You have done very well. I cannot tell you how much this birth pleases me."

Her smile is wide but there are shadows about her eyes. Belatedly, I remember that she laboured long and hard to give me my son.

"Are you well, my love?"

She starts slightly at the endearment, relaxing when she realises her job is over and she has fulfilled her promise to me. I reach for her hand, but her fingers are cold, her palm sweaty, and I draw it back again, surreptitiously wipe it on the sheet.

"I am tired, Henry. It was a hard travail that I feared would never end. I just need to sleep now."

I stand up, reluctantly pass my son back to his nurse, watching as she swaddles him again, trapping his arms, wrapping him tightly. He shrieks when his fist is removed from his mouth but after a few moments he closes his eyes and begins to suck on an invisible teat.

"Then you must sleep, Jane," I say, without taking my eyes from him, "and while you do so, I will put plans in place for the grandest christening this world has ever seen."

Placing my lips gently on her clammy brow, I try not to flinch from the aroma of blood and sweat that still clings to her. "I will return later on to see how you both are."

Prayers of thanksgiving are ordered, *Te Deums* are sung in every church, while cannons roar from the Tower and hogsheads of wine are distributed throughout the city.

As word spreads, England - the whole country - is illuminated with flames of joy. There are torches on every corner, bonfires in the streets, beacons lit on every hill as the news passes from city to city, town to town, hamlet to hamlet.

The king has his heir and England has a prince at last.

15th October 1537

Three days later and proclamations have been made across the realm, giving news of the prince's birth. Jane, still weary and abed, lost no time in sending out the announcement. The kings of Europe must take notice of me now. I am no longer the laughingstock. I have a son, a healthy, legitimate son.

Hampton Court is teeming with well-wishers; people come from all over Christendom to give my son their blessing. I make sure he is kept at a safe distance from them though, for contagion is always fatal to a newborn infant. He is secure in the nursery adjacent to the queen's chambers, and only a privileged few are allowed to look upon him.

I visit him each day, annoying the nurse when I lift him from his cradle, hold him in the crook of my elbow while we make plans for the ceremony. I even go so far as to consult him on the colour of his christening robe, and he gives me to understand his preference is for purple.

Mary, delighted with the gift of a new brother, receives the news of the prominent role she is to be offered in the proceedings with deep gratitude.

"You want me to be Godmother?"

She puts her hands to her face, so pleased that her cheeks turn a flaming pink. "Oh, what an honour that will be. Thank you so much, Your Majesty, thank you … Jane."

It is the first time Mary has accepted the queen's request that she use her given name. Jane has taken to Mary and in the brief time we have been married has become a sort of surrogate mother. I am glad of it. Mary is a plain, awkward girl and has the tendency to speak out of turn, sometimes sounding rude and unschooled in etiquette. Jane, ever polite and gentle mannered, will help to rectify that. She will add polish to the rough diamond of my daughter's demeanour.

"The other Godparents will include Norfolk and the Archbishop of Canterbury ..."

Mary's face falls, neither man being her particular friend. She has never forgotten how Norfolk dealt harshly with her in her youth, and Cranmer is keen for the new learning, something Mary abhors, even if she does try to conceal it.

Jane tightens her grip on Mary's hand.

"And, best of all, the king has given permission for Elizabeth to attend. She is travelling from Hatfield today and should be with us before supper."

Mary's smile returns. Despite the age difference, and all the trouble caused by Elizabeth's mother, she has a genuine affection for her sister. I wish I felt likewise but she makes me uneasy.

"That will be lovely," Mary replies. "All three siblings together for the first time. Elizabeth will adore her baby brother as much as I. I imagine in years to come this will be a day we will all look back upon gladly."

"Would you like to hold him again?"

Weakly, Jane beckons to the nurse, and she bustles forward with the child, places him in Mary's arms. A soft maternal glow settles on my eldest daughter's face, making her almost beautiful. Maternal. Perhaps Jane is right; perhaps she does need a husband and children to complete her. I suppose motherhood is a woman's right and purpose; it is after all what they are born to do. I must remember to speak to Cromwell and see what can be arranged.

When the time for the christening arrives, Jane is laid upon cushions, draped in velvet, and carried to a chamber from which the celebrations will take place. Of course, as is tradition, we will not attend the ceremony itself. It is Mary's task to oversee that. The queen and I will have no role but to wait here.

I can see Mary now, across the crowded room. She has taken hold of Elizabeth by the wrist and seems to be scolding her to keep still. The child can be difficult; those who care for her say she is often immoderate, pert almost. I hear reports of things she has said or done, sometimes they are amusing and make me chuckle, but often her actions cross the border between amusing and shocking. That, and her boundless energy, suggest she may take after me in many ways. If I were to spend more time in her company, I suspect she would become a favourite. Perhaps we can be friends, now there is no question of her entering the line of succession.

She has the same flaming red hair I had in my youth and also loves to dance and hunt. But there is always something about her that unnerves me. There have been times when I've caught a look in her eyes, and it is as if Anne has returned, for they are the very replica of her mother's and I fancy they burn with recrimination.

Nevertheless, despite my slight misgivings, Elizabeth is to bear the chrisom cloth, but since she is so young and flighty, her step-uncle, Edward Seymour, the elder of Jane's two brothers, is to carry her and ensure she behaves.

Jane did suggest that her other brother, Thomas, might be a better choice for he is good with children; he shares their love of fun, their sense of mischief. But, after some thought, I opted for Edward because Thomas cannot wholly be relied upon to behave any better than the children.

Immediately seeing my point, Jane agrees, swearing it is because he has never outgrown his own infancy.

"He was ever in mischief when we were children," she says, "and never took no for an answer. I doubt that will ever change."

Across the chamber, Thomas has relieved Mary by taking temporary charge of Elizabeth. He is currently discovering coins in the child's ears, making her squeal with delight at such confounding magic. If he keeps that up, he will be a pauper by the end of the day.

I grope for Jane's hand as, with much kerfuffle, the gathered nobles form themselves into pairs. Nobles, knights, chaplains, line up in order of hierarchy amid exaggerated politeness, ostentatious deference, and veiled insults passed off as banter.

And then my throat swells with emotion when the prince is carried in by the Marchioness of Exeter, his long velvet robe trailing over her arm, the ends borne by William Howard. The canopy above the boy's head is to be carried by Thomas Seymour, Bran, Carew, and Browne.

It is a sight I thought I'd never see. I watch my family with benign joy as Elizabeth is handed into the care of Jane's elder brother and, at last, the procession forms some semblance of order. Silently, feeling excluded from the proceedings, I watch them process from the room, leaving Jane and I alone.

We wait for a few moments, relishing the peace, and when I look down at her, I note her parchment complexion, the heavy shadows beneath her eyes. She is still exhausted.

"The ceremony will take quite a while. Get some sleep while they are gone. I will just sit here quietly."

She smiles gratefully and lays her head back on the pillows.

"Keep hold of my hand please, Henry. I like to feel you close by."

So, I sit and wait, one hand clasped in Jane's, the fingers of my other drumming my knee, impatient for my son's return. I will not rest easy until he is safely back in his nursery, away from all risk of contagion.

Together, the queen and I have decided upon the name of Edward. I shied from naming him Henry for I have used it so many times before. I spend a few moments pondering upon all my other sons, those who perished, some in infancy, some almost grown. Had they all lived, I'd have a small army of male Tudors. Why has it been so difficult?

Even Henry Fitzroi, my first surviving son, who so strong from birth did not live beyond his seventeenth year. Perhaps the name carries some ill luck; it has given me little joy. So, since this boy, my legitimate heir, was born on the Eve of St Edward, it seems appropriate he is so named. It also honours my grandfather, the warrior king, Edward IV, and to please Jane, her brother Edward, too.

Edward is a good name, a lucky name and, if prayers and hopes and self-sacrifice have anything to do with it, this child will thrive and grow to a man's estate. He will be provided with the best education, the best tutors, the best physicians that money can buy. I thank God there is time yet to teach him in the ways of kingship before … but I cannot think of my own passing.

That, God willing, is many, many years ahead.

Before that time comes, I will have at least a handful of sons. Jane has proven herself to be a strong fertile mother, and I was right to choose her, right to dispense with … Anne … and begin again. I was right and God's favour proves it.

I wake with a grunt and realise I'd fallen into slumber. My arm is cramped, my neck at an odd angle. I stretch out my leg, ease my head from side to side, a crack in my neck making me cry out. Jane starts up, suddenly. Her grip on my hand tightens and, when I gently pry myself free, she frowns and rubs her eye, dislodging her coif.

"Henry?" she smiles wanly. "Did I sleep very long?"

"Long and loud, you were snoring like a hound."

"Oh, I am sorry."

In all likelihood it was me who'd been snoring but, as usual, she fails to recognise my jest. She stretches her legs down the bed and winces at some unspecified pain. "Will they be back soon, do you think?"

"I think I hear someone coming now."

She fumbles for her kerchief and uses it to pat her lips and the small trickle of drool on her chin. Then she beckons for a cup and refreshes her mouth before relaxing back on her pillows, exhausted by the effort.

I wish she'd rally herself. Surely she can't still be so tired; it's been three days.

A herald enters the chamber and blasts an announcement, the noise making the queen wince. He is followed by Cranmer who halts just inside the door, stands erect and announces:

"Prince Edward, son and heir to the King of England, Duke of Cornwall and Earl of Chester!"

The procession re-enters the chamber, the sudden clamour after the peace seeming loud. The queen tries to pretend she isn't flustered but I note how rapidly she is breathing. I realise she is fighting for composure, but I know from experience she will overcome it.

She brightens a little when she spies the prince and lifts her arms, asking for her son. When she has Edward nestled to her bosom, she places her lips on his head, which is still damp from the font, and closes her eyes.

My son and his mother, a Madonna in the candlelight. I don't know when I've been so happy. I beam upon the company, with tears pricking my eyes.

19th October 1537

The next few days are spent joyously opening letters of congratulation from the heads of Europe. Gifts arrive, splendid, priceless offerings of gold, bolts of the finest silks and velvets, gold plate, jewels, horses and even a monkey with a golden collar. It is the congratulations from those enemies who merely masquerade as friends that please me most. It is gratifying to see them eat their words. They think I know nothing of the gossip concerning the king of England's infertility, his lack of prowess. I am glad to prove them wrong.

How Francis must be cringing at the news. I smile, imagine him squirming on his French throne as he dictates the words of congratulation, complimenting me on my son's perfections.

These small things fill me with joy.

When Brandon seeks an audience, we do not get to the matter in hand for almost an hour, as I insist that he listen while I read aloud the praise I have received for my son.

I have done it. I have succeeded. I have my heir. There is nothing further I need. What I wouldn't give for my father to be here so I could rub his nose in my success. But, of course, if he were, I'd no longer be king.

The next time I call in on the queen, I am gratified to discover she is sitting up and looking much brighter. She even allows me to feed her a few small slivers of her favourite quail and washes it down with good wine.

I climb onto her bed and she listens as I relate all the court news, for she is quite isolated here in her chambers.

I long for her to rejoin us at court.

"Once you are churched," I say, "we can take the prince on a short tour, show him off to the people a bit. They will enjoy a sight of him; they've waited long enough for a prince."

"Is he not a little young yet, Henry? Perhaps it would be wiser to wait until the weather grows warmer."

"Yes, I meant in the summer, of course."

I help myself to one of her quails, rip it in two and put a morsel on my tongue. Flavour floods my mouth. I eat another. Then I try to tempt her with a little lemon posset but, after a couple of small spoonfuls, she turns away. I finish it for her and then try the apple.

I lie back, clasp my hands on my chest, rest my head on the bedhead and give a discreet belch. I twiddle my thumbs; this bed rest is dull, and the sun is trying to shine. Perhaps I should take a turn around the garden. The spaniels haven't been out with me for a while. I rise from the bed, give Jane a quick kiss.

"I am glad you are feeling better," I say. "I will call in again after I've walked the dogs. Get some rest."

Her forehead is still clammy. She gives a smile and watches me go. At the door, I turn and wave and she waggles her fingers feebly in reply.

It is a fine afternoon and, as a consequence, I take the spaniels far further than I'd planned. We leave the garden perimeter and venture into the meadow, where the ground is claggy in places from the recent rain, the grass seeds clinging to my hose and the dogs' coats.

The world smells damp and chill, of rotting leaves, wet bark, decaying plants. Every so often, I pause to throw a stick and, with much barking, the dogs run to retrieve it. The tricky thing is persuading them to give it back. I lunge for the stick, but they dart away, barking like maniacs, far too fleet for me.

Cut goes down on his front legs, rear end waggling in the air, his tail like a banner. When I manage to grab hold of one end of the branch, a tug of war follows with me one end, the dogs the other. As we wrestle for possession I growl in ferocious mockery and in the end, I master them. Triumphantly, I wave the stick at them and, as I am about to hurl it across the park again, I notice a figure approaching.

Frowning, I stand and wait until he draws near.

"Cromwell! It is chilly out here. You are the last person I expected to see so far from his desk. Did I forget an appointment?"

He bows, the fine black cloth of his coat collecting as much grass seed as that of the dogs.

"No, Your Majesty. I come upon another, graver matter. The council sent me …"

He splays out his hands as if at a loss for words and I stop ruffling the dogs' ears and straighten up, so happy that I do not notice the first stirrings of dread unfurling in my gut.

"What is it? Has something happened to my son?"

"No, no, as far as I am aware the prince is thriving, Your Majesty. It – it is the queen I need to speak to you about."

"Jane?" I frown. "Yes. She is slow to rally but it was a hard birth and her first child …" I stop, floundering for words, for excuses, for reasons why she is not yet recovered but, somewhere deep inside, I know what is coming.

I know what his next words will be.

"The physicians, Sire … they are concerned that the fever has returned."

I draw back in denial.

"I was with her this morning. She seemed well enough. She even ate some quails and a lemon posset …"

As I speak, I recall that, in fact, she ate very little. It was I who enjoyed the lion's share of her meagre meal.

I look into Cromwell's sad eyes; note the furrowed brow, the beads of sweat on his upper lip. My head feels suddenly heavy, my neck droops and my shoulders collapse.

"Cromwell ... are you telling me the queen is going to die?"

I slump upon a fallen tree, the bark damp and rough, dead grass straggling about my knees. My heart, which a few moments ago had been buoyant, now feels like a leaden casket.

"We feel ... the physicians feel that you should prepare yourself for bad news, Your Majesty. I am so very, very sorry."

Like an infant, I plunge my face into my hands as sobs I cannot govern begin to shake my soul. I feel a hand on my shoulder, his voice as soft and comforting as a mother's.

"At least you have time to bid her goodbye, tell her of your love and gratitude."

I look bleakly across the dying meadow, the lank grass, the pewter-dark river that snakes away beneath the lowering branches of the oaks, and remember with awful clarity how I had begged God to grant me a son and offered Him 'anything' in return.

I see her just once more, but it is not the Jane I remember. She is lost so deep in fever that she doesn't know me. There are no smiles; her meek kind spirit has already died. She pulls her hand away, strains from me in some paroxysm of grief and sickness as she shrieks and curses.

"Jane," I say, "Jane, it is me. It is Henry." But she moans all the louder, transformed into some sort of demon. She calls for her mother, calls for her sister, calls for everyone but me. And I am the only one here. The only one who matters.

The one who needs her.

Her women are at a loss. When they try to soothe her, or place a cooling cloth upon her head, she flings them aside. She rages in a devil's tongue, her voice unrecognisable, her words incomprehensible, demonic, and terrifying.

This is not Jane.

Pushing her clamouring women aside, I back away, cast one more lingering look on the deathbed before fleeing from the bedchamber.

Like a wounded bear, I barge along the corridor, push through the weeping courtiers, burst through doors before the guards can open them and, at last, I dive into the silent sanctuary of my chamber.

In the centre of the room, I hang my head and stand panting, frantic with fear, angry at fate, and at God who has left me stranded again, rudderless in the raging river of life.

My breath issues in short gasps. *How can this be happening? Why is this happening?* Panic takes hold of me.

Suffocating, I grope toward the window, throw it open and stare blindly across the park. No, God, no! Not this. Please not this!

I cannot return to her bedside. I hate sickness. I dread fever and I fear death. There may still be life in Jane's body, but the woman I knew has already departed. That woman in the bed is not my queen. She has left me, just as my mother did. Just as Mary did. Just as … I am alone again. God has not blessed me after all.

24th October 1537

The very next morning, I quit Hampton Court and take refuge at Whitehall, where courtiers and servants creep around, their voices mute, their faces stricken. I send them from my presence, even my fool, so I might sit quietly in the darkened chamber. So that I might think.
But my thoughts are bleak.

Every one of my plans is laid waste. The great celebrations for the birth of our prince must now be muted in honour of his mother's passing. The Christmas season, planned down to the last word in the pageant, the last dance step, the last tumble of the jesters, must now be set aside.

This year, apart from the deference due to God, there will be no Christmas feasting at the royal court, no joy.

Not without Jane.

Her face wavers before me, and I am consumed with guilt for the numerous times I compared her looks unfavourably to other women, the times I despaired of her lack of wit, her simple, sombre sweetness, the times I wanted her to be more, more than what she was.

More than just Jane.

I see now that what she lacked in showy style she made up for with goodness of heart and, above all, fertility. She may have been weak, she may have been gauche at times, but she provided me with all I have ever wanted.

If only I had seen that before.

As I sit here alone, I fancy I hear sobbing. It is in my head, of course, my own sorrow at my own tragedy, the farce that is my life.

I imagine I hear Kate, her strong Spanish accents praying loud and emphatically for my late wife's soul and then, louder than that, so loud that it erases every other thought in my head, I hear Anne laughing; gleeful that all the curses she laid upon me are now come to pass and she has her vengeance.

The door opens, and I look up startled, expecting for a ghastly moment to see Anne standing there. Instead, a servant emerges from the shadows, places a tray at my elbow, pours wine into a cup.

I turn my head.

"I didn't send for that."

"Lord Cromwell ordered me to bring it, Your Majesty."

I nod but do not make reply. Cromwell. It is his way of making it known that he seeks an audience. He knows better than to disturb me himself, but I cannot face him yet.

I need to think about Jane.

Did I honestly love her? I told myself so but once we were married, the passion I felt for her while Anne was alive faded fast. I enjoyed the comfort she offered during the battle of my marriage with Anne. Jane provided softness after the brittle, warmth after the cold, water after thirst, esteem after scorn.

167

Had it not been for the discomfort of loving Anne, likely as not I'd never have noticed Jane, let alone made her my queen. My thoughts churn: they twist and tumble in my mind, the sorrow transforming almost unnoticed into something else.

Pain becomes anger.

Why, why, why does God punish me? Why has my life become one continuous queue of disappointments? Catastrophes line up, one after the other, ready to strike me, inflicting pain, drawing blood … *Tudor* blood.

The joy I'd taken at the kings of Christendom learning of my son's birth is now tarnished by the certainty that they will laugh when they are told I have lost my queen. At the thought of it, a jolt of fury charges through my body.

I knock over the cup; a red stain spreads across my hose, my knee chilling as the liquid cools. The curse that issues from my lips is foul, a blasphemy of the vilest kind.

I glance remorsefully up to Heaven and cross myself, send up a hasty prayer for forgiveness, but I fear I am too late.

He has already heard. Further punishment will follow.

When it grows too dark to see, I relent and allow Cromwell audience. He comes in as quietly as always, makes his bow and begins to offer his condolence. I raise my hand to shut him up and he falls silent.

"I do not wish to speak of it, Cromwell. I am not yet ready."

"As I imagine, Your Majesty, but there are arrangements that must be put in place."

"You can see to it. If you need instruction look back to my sister's funeral, she was the last queen to …"

I cannot speak the word, not yet.

"I looked in on the prince before I left Hampton Court. He is thriving, feeding well and his physicians are pleased with his progress."

"Good."

The last time I spoke with the royal doctors, they told me the queen was making good progress. Within hours of that statement, she was lost in fever, unable to recognise me, unable to speak coherently. No longer Jane. The next day, she was dead.

I hold up my hand again and Cromwell, who had been about to speak, closes his mouth.

"The prince must be protected. His household must be made secure. No visitors – we can't have anyone strolling in and out the palace at will. They must have written permission; permission from me, and no one else. Nobody from London is to go anywhere near his chambers, his servants and household are to be vetted, his health checked and double-checked; anyone showing signs of sickness must leave immediately – and I mean signs of a cold, not just plague. This boy was hard won. He is the most precious pearl in this realm, and children die, Cromwell, children die all the time."

I snarl the last few words through clenched teeth as the idea of losing my son takes possession of my wits.

My hands are shaking.

I look down at my clamped fist, relax it only long enough to grip his sleeve. My fingers claw into the velvet cloth, my rings glinting in the light of the fire. He waits for the fit to pass and when I feel steadier, I loosen my hold and he smoothes the fabric and looks into my eyes, flinching from whatever he discovers there.

"I am all too aware of that, Your Majesty, and all shall be done to ensure our prince's safety."

Of course, he knows. I have never forgotten how he lost his whole family to the sweating sickness. How does he manage to carry on, take pleasure in insignificant things, continue to nourish his earthly ambition, to care about matters of state, matters of faith?

I open my mouth to ask him, but his next words rob me of the unformed questions.

"Of course," he says, without looking at me. "Your Majesty realises the importance of remarrying as soon as possible? The prince needs a mother, and the country requires the security of another son … should anything …"

My jaw drops, disbelief growing like a mushroom in the darkness of my heart. I kick the side table away, the jug of wine, the plate of fruit crashing to the floor, malmsey splashing his fine new coat, apples and oranges bouncing across the chamber.

"Have you no pity? Get out of my sight, man!"

His eyes widen, his jaw flaps like a landed fish as he backs toward the door, gives a hasty bow, and flees from my presence.

The door closes and, for a little while, I stand and stare at it, astonishment and fury still pounding in my chest. Another wife indeed, and my last one only just passed.

I slump back into my seat, fumble for the cup before remembering it is upended near the wainscot. Another wife? I don't think so. Wives have brought me very little joy.

Darkness falls. I burrow into it so it muffles me, hiding my tears and concealing the grief that shakes my frame. I have never felt so alone but as I sit there, contemplating the sorry story that has become my life, I hear a sound.

A shadow steps from the deeper darkness and moves toward me. Her skirts hush across the carpet. I peer through the gloom, my heart racing as she draws nearer. The light from the window reveals the outline of a gabled hood against the sky. Is it the ghost of my mother? Or is it Kate come back from death to comfort me?

The figure reaches out, her great sleeves falling back to reveal long white fingers, a jewelled ring I do not recognise. Her hand falls gently on my shoulder, the blood frozen in my veins.

"Your Majesty?" The figure speaks. "I have come to see if I can offer you comfort."

I swallow the grief that sticks like a cancer in my throat and, with great daring, I reach for her. My fingers encounter warm skin, living flesh, not a ghostly form at all. I pull her down, so that she kneels at my feet, turns her pale face up to mine. Huge dark eyes, full of sorrow, not for herself, but for me.

For Henry.

"Anne?" I whisper. "How did you know?"

Her lips stretch into a smile, a tender gentle smile I've been craving.

"I am not sure," she says. "Some instinct brought me to you."

"I am glad of it, Mistress Basset," I reply. "For my heart is sore tonight."

To be continued in *A Matter of Time: the Dying of the Light* continue reading for an excerpt.

If you have enjoyed this book, please consider leaving a short review on Amazon and telling your friends about it.
Your support is so important to me.

Author's note

I have taken far too long to write *A Matter of Faith*. I had promised it would be available in early 2022 but here we are, in January 2023, and I am only just sending it off to my editor.

There were several reasons for this. The first being a contract to produce a non-fiction book for Pen&Sword publishers. This book will be called *How to Dress like a Tudor*, a history of fashion within the Tudor period plus hints and tips for those making their first attempt at sewing 16th century costume.

It took me far longer to put all the information together than I'd envisaged but I hope the resulting book will be a pleasing addition to my catalogue. There will be many colour plates, illustrating not just the clothes of Henry and the court but also those of the re-enactment group I am part of, *The Fyne Company of Cambria*.

While I worked on *How to Dress like a Tudor*, Henry was forced to take a back seat, something he wasn't at all happy about. Then, at the end of the summer, when I'd finally sent the non-fiction book to the publisher for edits, and I was finally free to get back to *A Matter of Faith*, my husband and I went down with Covid. For me, this ended up becoming long-Covid. I am still suffering a little with tiredness shortening my working day and forcing me to stop work early and take a nanna-nap.

Anyway, back to *A Matter of Faith: the days of the Phoenix*. This novel continues a few years after the narrative ends in *A Matter of Conscience: the Aragon Years*.

Henry has just managed to wriggle free from Catherine and is preparing to marry Anne Boleyn. The story, written from Henry's perspective, provides, as far as I am aware, a unique view of their relationship. Henry quickly becomes disillusioned, Anne fails to give him his son, and their mutual unhappiness is expressed through increasingly violent marital arguments. It is the original love/hate relationship and in the wings, of course, is Jane Seymour.

Jane has always been a bit of an enigma to me. Was she really the sweet, meek girl of popular history or something more? Perhaps her ambition was as great as her brothers', and her gentle manner masked a soul of steel. Just as in life, when she never really had time to make that clear, she remains somewhat unknowable in the novel. She leaves the reader guessing and you will have to make up your own minds. Whereas Anne is a clear mix of good and bad, as most people are, Jane is opaque, but she hasn't emerged as squeaky clean in this book. Whenever I tried to make her appear sweet, she'd stick out her stubborn-looking chin and say or do something surprising.

Henry's feelings for Jane are likewise impossible to determine. I like to dig beneath the surface and, despite him claiming she was the love of his life, I have my doubts. We know they married with almost obscene haste after Anne's beheading, but there is no hint of what the attraction may have been; they seem to have had little in common. The fact that we know so little about her probably accounts for the mild nature she has acquired in the popular mindset. Most of the women in Henry's life were either vitally intelligent or stunningly beautiful; I'd imagine he would prefer a mix of both. I can't imagine Henry being attracted to a dull woman. I apologise to Jane if she was in any way vibrant because I have not made her so. Although this book is fiction, to invent a wildly innovative Jane Seymour would have meant straying too far from the facts we do have.

We also know that after her death, the king mourned for quite a while and did not remarry for several years, but it was characteristic of Henry, or at least the Henry I have written here, to desire that which he could not have. Had she survived and given him sufficient time to tire of her, or had she not produced the heir he longed for, I think the outcome of the relationship may have been very different. It seems more probable that his request to be buried with Jane had more to do with her status as King Edward's mother than with love.

All the characters in this novel are based on historical figures, but they are fictionalised characters nonetheless. Henry may be among the most documented kings in history, but we only have his recorded actions and some wonderful letters. We know from those that he was passionate, romantic, and idealistic, but his innermost thoughts and motivations are hidden, and always will be. I had fun writing from Henry's perspective, but the real motivation for even his most unforgivable crimes will never be known. It is too easy to depict him as an out and out monster. I stopped believing in monsters a long time ago but I do believe that he would have found a way to excuse even his worst offences. He was an expert in self-forgiveness and has provided me with an irresistible opportunity to create a fabulously unreliable narrator of the events that took place during his reign.

It is my belief that Henry had an idealised image of himself that he consistently failed to live up to. He was a weak man in a strong body, a baby in a suit of armour, a cuddly teddy bear in a grizzly bear's suit. Initially, his intentions were good. He strove to be that 'perfect renaissance prince', but things beyond his control meant it didn't work out that way.

I don't think we can fully understand his need for a son; it had been instilled in him since childhood. Failure to produce a male heir was to fail both as a man and a king, and we shouldn't judge him from our 21st century perspective.

I think he craved love, not just that of a woman but of the people and, like a child, when he didn't receive it, he turned rogue. Craving the affection of a fertile woman but incapable of giving any real love in return, he rushed from one wife to another in search of the unachievable.

Of course, as I said earlier, we can only judge him fairly if we view his actions through the sensibilities of his day. It is easy, but very misguided, to judge his treatment of Catherine and Anne via the 21st century. It was not unprecedented for a queen to be asked to step aside to make way for a younger, more fertile woman but Catherine, quite understandably, was proud. It was only the English who were intolerant of female monarchs; Catherine's mother, Isabella of Castille, was a formidable ruler and, as far as Catherine was concerned, the rightful heir to Henry's throne was Mary, and she refused to consider any other option. No blame there.

Anne is a more complex matter. I hear many arguments about whether she set out to steal Henry from Catherine, but it doesn't sound likely to me. In the beginning, the most she could have hoped for was to become his mistress, a position she clearly didn't want. I don't think it would have occurred to her to hold out for a crown but, however she managed it, she did indeed become queen. Had she given Henry the son he wanted, the marriage may well have lasted. He'd turned the kingdom upside down and killed some of his closest friends to get her. Their relationship was not an easy one, but that is not uncommon and there are reports of loving interludes between them right up until the end. I tend to believe her position as queen was secure until she fell out with Cromwell. Most of us agree that Anne was innocent of the charges brought against her. When the dissolution of the monasteries began, Anne and Cromwell were in agreement, but once their ideas on church reform diverged, her status as queen became unstable. Perhaps if she had let Cromwell have his way, the arrests may never have taken place. The matter becomes even more interesting when you consider that the men who died alongside her were not only of similar opinion to Anne, but they were Henry's closest friends and influencers. They were also opposed to Cromwell. The two men arrested, Thomas Wyatt and Richard Page, who were later freed, were on good terms with him.

I think there is a possibility that Henry believed the charges. For all their differences, Anne was his beloved wife; he'd fought long and hard to marry her, turned the country upside down and destroyed some of his best statesman to do so.

The men accused of adultery with Anne were his friends; he drank with them, danced with them, hunted with them. They had formed a large part of Henry's life; both social and political. To someone as deeply insecure as Henry, the idea of his closest friends sleeping with his wife would have been personally devastating. A man like Henry, imagining himself cuckolded, would have acted swiftly, without due consideration and no doubt regretted it, just as he regretted beheading Cromwell a few years later.

Had Henry ever suspected that Anne had been executed erroneously, it would have been in character for him to ignore the matter completely and defy anyone to mention it, or her again. Which, of course, is exactly what he did.

Ask most people to describe Henry and they come up with things like 'obese', 'tyrant', 'monster', but these descriptions are not entirely fair. In his youth, Henry was athletic, loving nothing more than to hunt, play tennis, and joust. His enthusiasm for these things was matched only by his appetite, which, of course, didn't matter while he was active. After his accident, forced to give up or at least drastically reduce the sports he so enjoyed, he did not cut back on his customary diet. This doesn't make him greedy; it merely means he ate like a king. Had he continued to burn off the calories, obesity may have been avoided. It shouldn't be a sin to be obese and, as for greed, well, that can apply to skinny people too. I wonder if his actions would be so strongly condemned if he'd kept his youthful good looks.

We also tend to overlook the degree of pain he lived with. There were no effective painkillers, he had to grit his teeth and bear it. I know what I am like if I have a toothache, or my bad back is playing up. Living with severe, unmedicated pain would make anyone bad-tempered and this, added to the daily frustrations he faced, would be enough to make him appear monstrous.

It may sound as if I am apologising for Henry, but I am not. I am fully aware of his actions, but it is interesting to set aside preconceptions and reconsider his character. Of course, these ideas of mine may well be inaccurate, but it is the mindset I adopted while writing as Henry, in Henry's voice. When I am working, I shut myself off from the world, and he comes in, sits at my shoulder, and whispers his excuses into my ear. Sometimes, it is a very uncomfortable confession to listen to; sometimes, I pity him, often I hate him, but he never, ever, fails to be fascinating.

I hope, in some small way, I manage to provide the opposite point of view, an approximation of the complexity of Henry's mind.

If you are curious to see what happens next in Henry's trilogy, read on for an (unedited) excerpt from Book Three. A Matter of Time: Henry VIII, the Dying of the Light.

A Matter of Time:
Henry VIII, The Dying of the Light
Judith Arnopp

Late summer 1539 - Greenwich

I don't know how long I've been standing here, staring into the cooling darkness of her eyes. They slant slightly, her fine brows are arched and the nose is well-proportioned, in a kindly, heart shaped face.

She is perfect.

Her lips are pink, plump and kissable, her mouth curved upwards as if she is amused by the fools around her.

I 've no idea what all the fuss is about, she seems to say, but men compose sonnets in praise of her beauty. I have done so myself; my own lines, penned in the lonely depths of night when sleep was evasive, and I was ... filled with longing.

I've been in love with one woman or another since I reached manhood. First there was Kate, and when I tired of her Anne was waiting who, in turn, was usurped by Jane. I was not yet tired of Jane when she left me so soon after giving me my heart's desire – my son. I was not ready to lose her, and there was no woman waiting to take her place as my queen.

And according to my council, it is a queen I need.

I have an heir now but one boy is never enough, not for any king. They tell me a political match will not only secure the realm against the threat posed by the Holy Roman Emperor but will provide a brother for Edward. A Duke of York who will stand at his sibling's side in times of crisis – a younger stalwart brother such as I never had.

A curtain drifts in the movement of air when the door opens but I do not take my eyes from hers. I will make her my queen; she will warm my bed, she will soothe my aching need and she will strengthen the Tudor line. If anyone can give me strong sons it is she.

A footstep, a light touch upon my arm.

I turn, still dazed by the sight of Christina.

"Anne," I say, my voice husky from prolonged silence. "Is it that time already?"

I look about the chamber and realise it is no longer day; the sun is sinking, and night shadows are creeping across the floor. She smiles, pert and dark. Tantalising.

"The chamber is so dark, I thought at first there was nobody here and you were still with the council."

"No," I stretch my back, yawn and reach for my stick, turning at last from the portrait that has enthralled me for more than an hour.

Anne Basset looks reproachfully toward the painting.

"Is this the woman you will choose?"

Her face is clouded, and I realise with a small degree of satisfaction that she is jealous.

"Possibly. She is very handsome."

"And very young too."

"At sixteen, she is old enough."

I do not miss the hint of resentment in her tone and reach out for her. At twenty years old, it isn't as if Anne is yet in her dotage.

"They expect me to wed a foreign princess, Anne, or you know I'd take you to wife. I'd rather you than anyone else."

"So you say."

She pouts prettily, looks up at me through her lashes, prompting me to hook a finger beneath her chin and raise her face to mine.

I kiss the end of her nose.

"Don't spoil the evening with dissention. Supper will be here anon, and I want to play you a tune I've been working on."

Her arms slide about my waist, or as far as they can reach and she presses against me.

"Is it about me?"

I look down at her head, that reaches no higher than my chest.

"Of course it is, if your skin is softer than a new dawn, and your laughter merrier than a lark."

"It must be then."

She spins away from me, comes to a stop beside the painting.

"Very well, but can we draw the curtain over the portrait, so I don't have to put up with the Duchess glaring at me all through the meal."

"She doesn't glare."

She shrugs her shoulders and moves toward the supper table.

"It seems so to me. Perhaps it is because I mislike her."

I gasp, throw up my hands.

"She will someday be your queen."

Anne turns and smiles, tantalising dimples appearing on her cheeks.

"And when she is my queen, I will love her devotedly. I suppose you will arrange for me to receive a good position in her household."

"Of course. I wouldn't want you too far away."

She sits down, without waiting my permission and plucks a handful of grapes from the bowl, pops one into her mouth.

"I hadn't planned on becoming a king's mistress, Henry. I had hopes of a husband, a fine country estate and children ...plenty of sons."

She looks at me slyly as I take my seat at table, but I know her well enough by now to realise she is teasing. Even so, it is dangerous territory.

"And you have someone in mind? Tell me, who is this fine rich gentleman."

She cracks a nut, picks the kernel from the shattered shell.

"I've nobody at all in mind. I only have eyes for you, Your Majesty."

She is a saucy minx.

I open my mouth, about to parry her sarcasm with a sharp quip, but I am forestalled when the door opens and the servants troop in with supper.

The spaniels who have been sleeping at the hearth, pull themselves up and come to sit at my feet in the hope of scraps. I sit back and wait in anticipation while the dishes are uncovered, my mouth filling with saliva as the chamber fills with the aroma of roasted duck and capon. I help myself to one of each and Anne chooses a bird and begins to tear off strips of meat and place them on her tongue. She chews slowly, her eyes on mine.

"I do worry," she says, her eyes sliding away, "that the new queen will not show me favour once she learns of my ...position here at court."

Anne has no official position as royal mistress. She is just a girl who is good enough to offer her king comfort. I have no intention of drawing attention to that fact by endowing her with the office. I drop a stripped capon bone onto my plate and rinse my fingers, dab my lips.

"Nothing has been decided yet. I may decide not to marry Christina of Milan at all. I might decide to remain a bachelor, or I may decide to marry a wench from the royal kitchen. Whatever I decide will not be influenced in any way by you."

She drops her knife, a devastated expression flooding her face. She picks up a cloth, wipes her hands, straightens her back and clasps her fingers in her lap. Damn, I had not wanted a fight. Not with her. I reach across the table.

"Anne, come, come. I don't want to argue. Look at this lovely spread. Can we not just enjoy the evening? It is not often we have the chance to be completely alone."

Her eyes are awash with unshed tears. I sometimes forget how young she is, how unschooled in matters of the heart. After blinking them away, she lifts her chin and smiles blithely through her unhappiness.

That's my girl.

She retrieves her knife, and we begin to eat again, the silence broken only by the sound of Cut and Ball slobbering at a bone beneath the table. The evening is spoiled. Anne will try not to sulk, she will oblige me, but I know she will resent it.

I decide to reapproach the matter.

"You must try to understand. It is the council, not I who is keen for this marriage, and nothing is decided yet. There are other candidates and much negotiation to be dealt with before a decision can be made. Even then it will be months before the new queen arrives. It would be silly of us to worry about it now. We should enjoy ourselves while we can."

She nods but unenthusiastically. I can feel my temper growing short.

"Speak, speak freely. I will not mind what you say. Out with it!"

She puts down her knife, picks up her wine cup and rinses her mouth, licks her lips.

"Very well."

She looks at me directly, unflinchingly. "I understand that you are to remarry, I understand the reasons why it can't be me, but it will be hard for me to relinquish you. Oh, I know you say, you want me close by, and you will continue to visit me when you can but ..."

Her eyes fall to her lap, I notice her chin wobbling. She is trying very hard not to cry. I reach out and place my hand on top of hers. She takes a deep breath and finishes her sentence all in a rush. "How will I bear it, thinking of you lying with her where I have lain, knowing the jokes you will share with her, the things you will do with her, the fancy little love tokens you will bestow upon her. The pretty poems you will write for her ...How can I know all that and still be civil? How can I tolerate her being hailed by all and sundry as your queen when it could be ... Look at her, Henry, she is beautiful. I can never compare! I would not be human if I were not jealous."

She stops suddenly, lowers her head, realising how far she has overstepped the margins.

"Anne." She looks up and we stare at one another, unblinking.

"As I said, I may not marry her at all. There is another, preferred by Cromwell for her Lutheran connections. Her brother, the new Duke William, is part of the Schmalkalden League and an alliance with him will bolster our defence against Spain and France. You see, my personal preferences are not considered; it is all about politics, my dear."

She frowns into a wine cup and waves a hand toward the now covered portrait of Christina.

"But that has nothing to do with this one. She is related to the King of Spain, why are you even considering her?"

Anne is very well informed. I wonder who has been enlightening her. She is right, of course, Christina is not the best political choice. Besides that, she has refused me and aligned herself with ... but I am not going to admit to that. It is simply that I can't seem to stop looking at her image; it does no harm to imagine her in my bed. She would be so perfect. My mind slips way, recalling the soft hue of her painted cheek, the moist promise of her lips …

Anne clears her throat, bringing me back to the present. I smile, lean over the table and take her hand again.

"I am not considering her. Cromwell has made it clear where my duties lie, and envoys have already been sent to Dusseldorf to sound out the idea of an alliance between me and the Duke of Cleves' sister."

She frowns.

"And her name is?"

"Anne. Her name is Anne."

I am plagued by Annes.

Author Biography

When Judith Arnopp began to write professionally there was no question as to which genre to choose. A lifelong history enthusiast and avid reader, Judith holds an honours degree in English and Creative writing, and a Masters in Medieval Studies, both from the University of Wales, Lampeter.
Judith writes both fiction and non-fiction, working full-time from her home overlooking Cardigan Bay in Wales where she crafts novels based in the Medieval and Tudor period. Her main focus is on the perspective of historical women from all roles of life, prostitutes to queens, but she has recently turned her attention to Henry VIII himself.

Her novels include:
A Matter of Conscience: Henry VIII, the Aragon Years. (Book one of The Henrician Chronicle)
A Matter of Faith: Henry VIII, the years of the Phoenix (Book Two of The Henrician Chronicle)

The Beaufort Bride: (Book one of The Beaufort Chronicle)
The Beaufort Woman: (Book two of The Beaufort Chronicle)

The Kings Mother: (Book three of The Beaufort Chronicle)

The Heretic Wind: the life of Mary Tudor, Queen of England
A Song of Sixpence: The story of Elizabeth of York
Intractable Heart: The story of Katheryn Parr
The Kiss of the Concubine: A story of Anne Boleyn
Sisters of Arden: on the pilgrimage of Grace
The Winchester Goose: at the court of Henry VIII
The Song of Heledd:
The Forest Dwellers
Peaceweaver.
Her non-fiction articles feature in various historical anthologies and magazines and an illustrated non-fiction book, *How to Dress like a Tudor* will be published by Pen & Sword in September 2023

For more information:
Webpage: www.judithmarnopp.com
Author page: author.to/juditharnoppbooks
Blog: http://juditharnoppnovelist.blogspot.co.uk/